The
Path
ALONG THE WAY

Stories, Inventions, Incidents, and Encounters

Along A Long Life

KENNETH A. SYMINGTON

Rushmore Press LLC
www.rushmorepress.com
1 888 733 9607

PREFACE

When I was an adolescent, maybe about 12 to 13 years old, I became an avid reader of books covering a wide range of subjects. Two books that I remember as having had a great effect on me were the works of Marguerite Yourcenar, and of Jose Enrique Rodo', both excellent authors with very sensitive psychological perception. Here are two short quotes from the latter:

> *"While we are alive, there is nothing in us which doesn't suffer change or modification. Everything is revelation, everything is a teaching, all is hidden treasure in things; each day the sun brings out sparks of originality. And everything is, within ourselves, as time goes by, the need for renovation, to acquire new force and light, to become aware of the bad not yet perceived, to enjoy the good not yet felt; to prepare, finally. our adaptation to conditions as yet unknown to experience."*

"For whoever feels the need for an intimate reform, who has to break a habit or inclination which holds his moral personality prisoner; for whoever sees his energies known to him exhausted, the complex and variable character of our nature constitutes a welcome promise of change and regeneration."

About that same time, I started writing down in longhand (there were no computers then) in a notebook, any quotes that I found interesting or meaningful to me, as well as any thoughts I was having at that time, that were either stimulated by those quotes. or generated within my own mind by events that were happening to me in my life, or by encounters with people during that time, or by books that I had read.

This I continued haphazardly during my lifetime, and now that I have reached the upper limits of seniority, I find myself with a large collection of notebooks, which in effect sort of narrate the experiences of a lifetime, and the ideas that stimulated me along the way.

The items I noted down were often quotes from known authors that I found challenging or interesting to me as guideposts, and I have identified in this volume the origin and exact provenance of each piece of writing. They are not selected at random; they are listed here because they were really important in my life, at a specific time, and in forming and shaping my judgement, my personality, and my view of the world.

They have been guideposts which I actively and purposefully used to shape, form and guide parts of my life, which I have returned to at pivotal moments of my life. They constitute, so to speak, "a part of me". Unfortunately I was not careful in jotting down the exact origin of a few of them, so if a particular quote is written down without identifying its author or origin, I must apologize to the author for my carelessness. They had a crucial effect upon my life. Be assured that in any case their quote was important and meaningful enough to become a signal "guidepost" in a man's development (mine!). I am thankful to them, and quote them because I hope this particular habit of collecting similar items may be also used by others who are following their own collected quotes.

Although this book has some stories that in reality happened to me, the book is not a biography, or story of my life. In it I have gathered a random collection of not only significant quotes, but also stories that I have heard or imagined or invented, myths from different cultures, dreams or nightmares that I have had in the course of a long life, that I have found to worthy of being preserved, sly jokes that I have borrowed from others, anecdotes, things I have heard......... that again ....may have been real or imagined, incursions into possible hypotheses, descriptions of places I have visited, in this world or another one, and anything that I have heard from others which I did not wish to forget, and finally perambulations of my own imagination. The quotes have been very important in my life, because they have been to me much more than a simple group of words to provide thought or entertainment. They are thoughts that I have actively tried to incorporate into my own life decisions. and use them to guide my actions. This book is not a dictionary, but is more like an "ideary", a collection of ideas: mine and others'.

THE FIVE STAGES OF LIFE

Looking back upon my life at this advanced stage, 87 years old, I believe I can clearly see it divided into five more or less separate and very distinct stages, each with its own qualities, characteristics, and results. I have therefore composed this volume following these five stages in order, writing down events, stories and sayings I came across at each stage. I wonder if that division in stages might be the same or roughly equivalent in the lives of other men as well? At any rate, to me, those stages seemed to develop as follows:

I.- Childhood (Ages 1-10)

II.- Adolescence (Ages 11-20)

III.- Experimentation (Ages 20-40)

IV.- Fullness (Ages 40-75)-

V.- Seniority Ages (75 +)

The text of this book follows these five stages in the order in which they appear to have taken place in my particular life:

JULIAN FELLOWES

"The danger of beauty in the very young, is that it can make the business of life seem deceptively easy"

I

CHILDHOOD
(1932-1942)-(Age 1-10) (Havana, Cuba)

Under the best conditions, and in a family that is caring, protective, and not abusive, giving careful guidance and example to a child, this can be a very happy, memorable and productive period in a lifetime. This was happily my case, although I am aware that when those favorable conditions do not apply, for whatever reason, early childhood can be hellish period for a growing child, leaving indelible negative marks, often for a lifetime. I remember my childhood as a happy time, playing a lot, going to beaches, learning to swim, and running around with playmates of my own age. School was interesting, I generally had good teachers, and I was learning grammar in both Spanish and English versions. This caused some confusion in my mind and I sometimes wondered what I really was, English or Cuban (my father was English and my mother Cuban). The positive side of that was that I was really exposed to not one, but two cultures, a particularly desirable situation because it enriched my perspectives and widened my horizons. I was never physically punished and was always treated well; not to say that bad behavior was tolerated: it wasn't, but again I was mostly a well behaved boy.

One exception in this happy picture is that I, as well as most boys of that age at that time, was subjected to the occasional hazing and abuse that older boys in school were prone to exercise upon the younger boys, mostly behind the backs of teachers. But even that, I think, was useful in that it made me realize that all was not good and beautiful in the world, and I should better prepare myself and learn how to deal with it; and I did.

When I was about 8 years old, I clearly remember having made a forceful pronouncement, on one of our family conversations, with parents, uncles and aunts present, that I was "never to have a child in my life!" This caused some merriment, and consternation, coming from a young child. My mother tried to say that one could never forecast that kind of future. As a matter of fact, it was a forecast that came about, because I never had a child and certainly never wished to have one. While I have nothing against others having children, I am quite happy to have had none, and have never regretted it.

How to be Safe

When I was about 3-4 years old, my family had employed a live-in maid who had a room in our house and was assigned a number of household duties, one of which was to take care of me when I was left alone in the house for whatever reason. She was a middle aged lady who had been born in a small, isolated farm in the countryside, and had never been exposed to life in city or received any formal education. She was, however a very pleasant woman, with good manners and a good heart. Because of the background where she was born, she had not heard or become accustomed to the occasional loud alarm sound emitted by passing police cars on a chase, or by ambulances carrying a sick person to a hospital. That loud sound terrified her, and her reaction to it whenever she heard it, was to run for cover and hide, ...of all places,...... under the bed in her room, and whimper there in full terror until the sound had died away.

Since I spent a lot of time with her as a very young boy, of course I imitated her reaction and promptly followed under the bed thinking that it was safe and proper thing to do. That went on for a while until I grew older and began to realize that there was no reason for her terror, and stopped imitating her actions. I laughed when I remembered how silly I had been in following her loony movements.

Early impressions in life seem to have some very lasting effects, because even later in life, whenever I heard a police or ambulance alarm, I had an involuntary twinge of fear. Even though I no longer react to it then, or run for cover, the sudden, instantaneous, passing fear reaction remains to this day.

So......how to be safe?...........just run and hide under your bed!

A FAILED HERO

When I was growing up as a boy, in a large family house with uncles and aunts living with us, a particular uncle, my mother's brother aroused my interest and affection. He was intelligent and well educated. Eventually when he was of the right age, he decided to go to Paris and study medicine at La Sorbonne, then, as now, a pre-eminent university in the world, specially good in their medical schools for training doctors. That aura of having gone away to Paris, significantly increased in my view the respect and near adoration that I built up for this absent uncle. He was gone for a good eight or nine years, after which one day he announced he was coming back home to practice medicine in our city. Our household was quickly, happily upset with his coming and the family even added a brand new room to the house to lodge him. As a child I was naturally eagerly awaiting to receive my hero.

He did arrive, to much celebration, and then settled to a routine of teaching and medical practice.

The problem was that I soon realized he had very little interest in my boyish life at all, and avoided my company, and in time I discovered that he had secretly spoken to my mother behind my back, objecting to some of my behavior, which was perfectly normal for a boy my age, and went even as far as to tell her how she should bring me up. I was very hurt and wounded by my hero's actions, and thereafter always avoided his company by acting gruff and unfriendly, which caused of course more of his complaints against me. I never allowed him in my trust again.

A number of years later, he decided to move his wife and family to a town in New Hampshire. Many years passed without my contacting him, but at one point I was going to college in the New York area, and all of a sudden I decided to call him and see if I could come visit him and forget all past resentments. So I called the phone number I had for him His wife came to the phone and I explained to her the reason for my call. To my utter surprise she informed in a very cold and disinterested voice, that my uncle was a very, very busy man, and that they could not afford to spend the time receiving me. The impression she left with me was that I should never call them again.

Even though that shocked me, I realized I should have expected that behavior from people like them.

But I had learned a very important life lesson, which I have put in practice ever since: **do not ever come close to, or cater to any people that do not have equal respect for you.**

What a Queen!!
Elizabeth I of England

England was about to be invaded by the Spanish Armada in 1588, and Queen Elizabeth I was determined to fight to the end to avoid the invasion. She went to Tillbury on the coast, where her troops were awaiting the arrival of the Spaniards, and addressed them in these incredibly rousing words; her speech was longer, but below are the most meaningful and brave words

"I am come amongst you, as you see, at this time not for my recreation and disport, but being resolved in the midst of the heat of battle to live

and die amongst you all. Or lay down for God,
my kingdom and for my people, my honor, and my
blood, even in the dust. I know I have the body of a
weak and feeble woman, but I have the heart and
stomach of a King, and a King of England too, and
I think it foul scorn that Parma or Spain or any
Prince of Europe should dare to invade the borders
of my realm.".

What a speech from a queen!.

No wonder the Spaniards lost the battle, were dispersed in the ocean and never could invade England.

ON ANIMALS

A very unpleasant incident took place when I was about 4 years old; it marked me for life.

My large family lived in a two story house with a patio and back yard which had a tall fence of iron bars at the back which separated it from our neighbor's property facing the next street behind us. One could see through the iron bars an open garden with grass and trees, and at the end, the neighbor's house.

In that yard they kept a female pig that roamed about the open space. She was usually quiet and made no noise.

One day I heard a huge commotion coming from that space, and as I ran out to see, I watched two unknown men, hired by the neighbor to kill the pig for cooking it. It was usual at that time and place to roast pigs over a grill with charcoal, their body pre-seasoned and slit open along the breast and belly and hind quarters. What I did not immediately realize was that there was an idea loose at that time, that pigs would taste a lot better when cooked, if they had been killed by literally beating them with clubs over their whole body until they died from hemorrhaging and the blows to their heads. This is what the two men proceeded to do, right in front of my view. The pig of course was squealing very loudly, trying to avoid the blows. This lasted quite a few minutes until it finally expired and was taken away. I was driven to distraction and was loudly crying myself, begging my mother to do something to stop that awful sight, but there was not much she could do except call the police, which arrived too late anyway.

The incident made a very big impression on me. Up to that time, I had always been fond of animals: the dogs, cats, and birds we had at home.

But after that incident, I reached a conclusion that I have strictly kept all of my life, even to this day: to never willingly hurt any animal, to protect them, be kind to them, to love them, and not allow anyone in my presence to hurt them.

All through childhood, we had a big backyard (in another house) in the outskirts of town, and I remember having not only dogs and cats, but also several roosters and hens, a cage with many white passenger pigeons free to fly out of their cage and return as they wanted, another cage with some 6-8 rabbits, a canary in his own cage, and even a small non-poisonous snake.

The love and care of animals thus became an important factor in my life and remains so to this day, when I have a small, totally spoiled, female cat to keep me company. She sleeps with me, and her favorite position is to lie by my side, resting her head on the open palm of my hand extended beside her, for hours at a time.

Another bad experience with animals happened during the time I was attending college in upper New York State: a college friend invited me to spend a Christmas vacation with him at his family home in the country. His family was a farming and animal-breeding family, very close to their farm and not very educated or polished. His father welcomed me for the holidays, and I believe made up his mind to show me "the real life at the country"----"how real men live"—"none of that sissy city living" etc. So he decided to take us hunting deer, arming us with rifles and going out into the forest to hunt deer. I felt I could not refuse the invitation. I had never used a gun and basically didn't know what we were doing. Sure enough we saw a deer and he rapidly pointed it out to me, urging me to take aim and fire, which I did, but with my total lack of experience, I only hit the poor deer in his leg, not killing it, while it proceeded to painfully limp along into the trees as best he could. My friend's father then took a second shot and finished off the poor beast, which we then took to his home and proceeded to open it, quarter it, and prepare the meat for future dinners. He insisted that I be present throughout this whole operation, because he had to show this "city boy" how life was lived in the country. We actually had a portion for dinner in the next day or two. I was so depressed by seeing what I had done to the defenseless animal, that the experience reinforced my prior determination to always avoid hurting animals under any conditions in my future.

So the terrible experience of witnessing the pig's and the deer's death was one reason why that reinforced my feelings as an animal-loving person. The good came out of the bad, and I have loved animals before and ever since.

A LIMERICK FROM BOYHOOD

At the time of my boyhood in the late 1930's, there was a very popular refrain, sung by children in Cuba to a very familiar, rhymed tune. What was amazing is that it really referred to real events that took place in Spain in 1709, more than two centuries before! Why we kids in Cuba were singing a rhyme that referred to an event so far past in history is a mystery. Of course we could not have possibly known what those events were. The actual source appears to have come from the time of Queen Anne of England, when an early Duke of Marlborough was fighting in the War of Spanish Succession between France and England where the French mistakenly believed that John Churchill (then Duke of Marlborough) who was fighting the French, had died. The song became popular in France in the times of Louis XVI when one of the dauphin's maids sang it, which pleased the kings, and soon became known throughout Versailles and the rest of France. It reached Spain through the influence of the Bourbons, with the name Marlborough reduced to a more pronounceable "Mambru'" in Spanish.

There are versions of the same song in other languages. The English one is sung to the words "For He Is a Jolly Good Fellow". There are similar Spanish versions sung is Argentina, Chile. Mexico, Paraguay, Peru, Uruguay and other Latin American nations. Beethoven used the musical theme in his composition "The Victory of Wellington"

The refrain is shown below. Of course the children in Cuba had no idea of its true meaning, history, background or people it referred to. We could not pronounce the "Marlborough" properly, so the name came through phonetically as "Mambru". Here it is:

> "Mambru' se fue a la guerra
> montado en una perra
> la perra se mato'
> y Mambru se revento'
> que dolor, que dolor, que pena
> Mambru' se revento'"

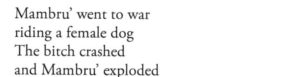

> Mambru' went to war
> riding a female dog
> The bitch crashed
> and Mambru' exploded
> what a shame, what a shame, what a pain
> that Mambru' burst open.

The above version was apparently a local popular, mistranslated, and Cuban distortion of the original Spanish version which went (in English);

> Mambru' went to war,
> what pain, what pain, what a shame
> Mambru' went to war,

Don't know when he will return
Do-Re-Mi, Do-Re-Fa
Don't know when he will return

THE PATRIARCH.- A SHORT STORY

It was during the late 1880's, a time quite different from the present, when customs, traditions, and behavior followed a pattern very different from the present, and it took place in a country town not far from the capital, but far enough to retain most of the usual behaviors from centuries past.

He was a forceful landowner and manager with firm convictions about life and how to live it, and no compunctions about letting others know about those convictions and expecting them to follow them as well. He and his wife had a number of children, including three girls and several boys. One of the convictions he had no trouble in often expressing to his daughters, was his idea that their function in life was to take care of him as he got older. This implied as well that he expected them to remain single and unmarried, because as married women they could not devote their time to their proper function of taking care of him, in his view.

His instructions apparently landed in fertile soil in the case of his two younger daughters, because in spite of several affairs they had with promising husband candidates, they actually never married and for whatever reason remained single. This was not the case with his older daughter who was made of more solid fiber and who refused to follow his expectation. She was also smart and guessed what was the right way to handle the situation, so she discreetly went to visit her aunt, who was married to a justice of the Supreme Court and gently explained the problem to him, and he agreed to talk to her father and politely suggest io him that he was making an excessive and improper demand to his daughter, and that he should allow his daughter's marriage, who had already met her future husband through a family connection. She brought him home to be introduced to the patriarch, who surprisingly, faced with circumstances and opposition he could not overcome, knew better than to oppose his stubborn daughter and the justice's request, and proceeded to welcome his future son-in-law with full courtesy. The marriage took place shortly thereafter, and family relationships settled down to peaceful coexistence.

The irony about the end of this story is that in fact the old patriarch died at a young 49 years of age from a stroke, and never lived long enough to need to be taken care of by any of his daughters. His early demand upon them turned thus to be ineffective and unnecessary. So much for how to deal with stubborn, old codgers.

II

ADOLESCENCE
(1943-1952)-(Ages 11.20)

This can be described as a very challenging period for most of us, because during that period we are exposed to all sorts of new experiences, we meet many new people, we wake up to sexual feeling for the first time, decide what we would like to study or what profession/occupation we tend to prefer, settle down on preferences on people, clothes, events, happenings, music. It was certainly difficult for me! It can be a very trying period. We do not yet have the experience upon which to make those choices, at that age, and we often make equivocal ones, unless we especially have some helpful guidance, or are sharp enough to tell the differences. It is a period which often settles things for a long time in the future. It can be exciting and interesting, but there is always a high probability of unwelcome events happening. One of the key incidents that tend to happen during that period is our <u>encounter with sex</u>.

I had an early, non-consummated, sexual experience that happened at home, where we had a big family including uncles and aunts living in a large house big enough to accommodate all of us, and employing a live-in cook and maid. I must have been about 11 years old, with no experience in sex other than the self-pleasuring actions that most kids of that age engage in. The cook was a woman of about 30 or so, and one day I inadvertently sauntered into her room and found her totally naked, about to enter the bathroom to rake a shower. She blushed but smiled at the same time, which incited my curiosity and I moved closer and eventually we ended up in her bed, with her naked next to me and I fondling her breasts and genitals. This went on for a short time, when a sudden noise nearby startled us and we thought someone was coming by, so we ended our contact. We did not ever repeat our encounter, because I believe the noise we heard was my mother coming near, and she must have seen or suspected what was going on, so shortly thereafter the cook was let go, and that was that. Everything considered, not a bad first contact of that kind, although I felt sorry for the cook. After that, I had my first two full sexual encounters (with a female, and with a male) when I was about 13 years old. It should be mentioned that either because of heritage, or because of doing lots of exercise at an early age, I had developed a physical body that looked much older than I really was. The photographs taken of me at that time show a young man that could easily pass as being 21 years old, and yet I was only 13; so people frequently and naturally mistook me as being a much older person. This was accentuated, as I mentioned above, by the fact that I was generally very serious and acted and spoke with a more serious tone that was expected from a 13 year old boy.

Some classmates at school began to converse about sex, which none of us had had any direct experience with, and the older brother of one of them decided that he was going to introduce 3 or 4 of us into having our first sexual experience, whereupon he took us to one afternoon to one of the many brothels existing at that time in a certain section of Havana, intended to serve not only nationals, but especially the many foreign tourists that visited the town. We were all extremely curious and excited, so we proceeded to go with him to visit the place, which was really nothing but a private home in the old section of town, with a living room, dining room, kitchen and patio on the main floor, and bedrooms and bathrooms on the upper floors.

We entered the base floor living room and sat down in the chairs and sofas arranged there, first paid our monetary "dues "and soon of a few scantily dressed women came into the room, and paraded in front of us in provoking stances.

The procedure was this: one had to choose the one you wanted, whereupon she would then lead you upstairs to a private bedroom with an ample bed and an adjacent bathroom. There you accomplished the deed, which I was able to perform without any difficulty, and was over and done within a matter of about one half hour, after which you cleaned up and proceeded to join your classmates below, all of us gloating, of course, about how well we had "performed" and how "satisfied" we had left our respective lady partners.

I remembered that during my "performance" my partner in crime asked me: "This is your first time with a woman, isn't it?" To that I replied with a slightly superior tome: "Oh no! I have done this many times before!" I doubt very much that she believed me. At about the same age, I had my first sexual experience with a man. It happened while I was attending an open air book fair, with kiosks set up in an open park, each selling books of all kinds, a periodic event taking place in town. As I wandered around the kiosks, I noticed a young man (he must have been about 21) came up next to me and made a comment, asking me if I had read one of books set in the display in front of us. I answered him, and this led to a pleasant conversation about books and authors. We compared authors we liked and disliked, and as a consequence, continued conversing as we walked down one of the avenues nest to the park. He was a very intelligent and good-looking young man, and he of course took me to be about his equal in age, as usually happened. After pleasantly walking about and conversing, he mentioned that a friend of his lived very close by and would I like to go visit him for a bit (I suspect it was his own house). After thinking about it for a few minutes, I agreed to go, and we soon mounted the steps to a pleasant house, sat down, and continued our conversation (his friend was not in). Our conversation soon turned into an open seduction of me, moving to the bedroom and having full sex, my first time with a man, where I played the male (top) part. As I remember, it was on the whole a very pleasant and satisfying experience, and I very much enjoyed his company. He wanted us to meet again, but it was my first time, and I was uncertain and confused about my feelings, did not know what to say or plan, so I demurred, and in fact never saw him again. Perhaps, in doing so, I may have lost an opportunity for an important and life-long friendship.

A DECLARATION OF INDEPENDENCE

At about 12 years old, I believe in most cases, boys leave their state of happy (or unhappy) boyhood and begin to feel and see the world in a somewhat different light, which is characterized by feeling more self-assured and decisive, and rejecting parental influence and control. I definitely felt that at the time and my strategy was to limit contact and not follow parental instructions, as far as it was possible to evade them. I employed my "taciturnity" in avoiding normal contact, conversation, and interchange and become isolated, limiting my conversation with parents and family to the minimum. This was noticed, especially by my mother, who started to complain gently that I was being anti-social and that I should try to become more accessible. She was quietly and gently pursuing these suggestions, never in an objectionable or violent way. These urgings I steadfastly refused and became more and more introverted. It was really a very positive departure from daily parental control, when a boy begins the needed process of individuation and formation of his personality. This process continued during my adolescence until its purpose was achieved. Later on in my life, I restarted very cordial relations with my mother, and enjoyed her company, but never putting with any of her excesses, such as when she would go on about something like the beneficence and the goodness of certain persons for example,. I would laugh at her credulity, and made her join me in the laughter. It very much affected me when she eventually died at an age close to 10 0 years, after a short illness. I lamented her passing, while realizing how good a mother she had been to me. Her character was evident when you considered that both her parents had died quite young, ages 49 and 51, leaving her in charge of family of five other younger sisters and brothers, while having received no prior preparation or instruction for the job, and then succeeding in making the family survive and prosper in the following years.

PERSEVERANCE

One can look at perseverance generally in two ways: a positive one is to consider perseverance in pursuing an objective to be a desirable quality in the midst of life's conundrums, because if one sets one's sights on something worthwhile and pursues it until achieved, that can be a "good" thing. On the other hand, stubbornness in dealing with anything, blindly refusing to hear or consider anyone else's opinion or evident facts, can lead to failure and disaster. In my case, using steadfast perseverance led me to an ambiguous conclusion that could be taken in more than one way.

This had to do with the business of going to college.

Like most of us high school graduates, we had to select at 17 what subject to major in at college, and more importantly, where to do it, namely, in what college. This is a major decision for any adolescent, because upon it is formed the map of his whole future working career, money-making activity, and personal satisfaction; and that decision must be made at the tender age of 17.

The problem is compounded by the fact that at age seventeen, we really do not know much about careers or about colleges; we do not have the facts, know the places, or have much concept about what any career would be like. Yet, the decision must be made. So at seventeen, after some consideration, I decided that I wanted to study Chemical Engineering, based only on some basic experiments in chemistry I had been exposed to in high school and before. In considering colleges, I had perused some college catalogues from American universities, and decided to apply to 4 of them: Cal Tech, (MIT) the Massachusetts Institute of Technology, Cornell, and Rensselaer Polytechnic Institute. All of them were top class schools with justified reputation. To my gratified surprise, I was accepted in all of them (I had very good high-school credits), except by Rensselaer, from whom I received a letter from its Director of Admissions, telling me that they were unable to accept me. This was not only a surprise, but also a cause for great anger on my part: how DARE they refuse me! On what basis? For what reason? The letter gave no reasons. I became so angry that I decided to call the Director of Admissions on the telephone several times insisting on his receiving me in person to discuss my admission. He finally relented, came to the phone and we set up an appointment date and time for me to come in person to Troy, New York, where Rensselaer is located. This was in 1949, and I was living then in Havana, Cuba. At that time there was no airplane service between the US and Cuba (this was before the age of commercial passenger planes), so one had to go by ship from Havana to Miami, then by train from Miami to Troy in upstate New York, a trip of about 1 ½ days long each way. I proceeded to take the trip and arrived in Troy for my meeting with that illustrious director. I was shown to his office and presently he came in and sat down: he was a man well into his 60's or 70's and not very alert, I noticed. Upon reviewing my application, after some mumbling, and my questioning, he went on to advise me that in the past, they had only accepted applicants who had graduated from LaSalle High School, a Catholic high school in Havana. I myself had graduated from an equally qualified and respected St. George's School, a non-religious school. This exasperated me to the limit, and then I asked him whether Rensselaer accepted <u>only</u> students from Catholic high schools, or <u>only</u> from LaSalle High Schools? After some hemming and hawing, he emphasized that this was not the case, whereas I pointed out with equal emphasis, that his record did not show that in practice, and that he was not telling me the truth, and that in any case that if he persisted in denying me admission, I would like to talk then to the President of Rensselaer about this. He then retracted and told me that in my case I <u>would</u> be admitted to Rensselaer in the following semester, and gave me a letter of acceptance before I left his office.

So, perseverance did pay off in this case, and I gloated about it, because Rensselaer was and is an excellent school, providing a top level technical education, among the best in the country. I have no regrets in graduating from that university, and have found it extremely helpful in my subsequent career.

Now, here comes the ambiguity: Rensselaer is located in Troy, New York, which was a developing industrial center in past centuries; at the time I was there, however, it was a poor, ugly town that had been long by-passed by the industrial wave as it went westward and beyond in the 1800's. The buildings in the city were old and decaying, there was very little or no cultural activity going on, and no special artistic or theatrical institutions there except Rensselaer. It was not a pleasant city to live in, although living in the campus itself, we were somewhat removed from the city itself.

Had I instead been less "persevering" (or stubborn?), and accepted my admission to CalTech in Southern California, I would have enjoyed an ideal climate, enticing beaches and mountains, and a much more experimental environment; things Troy never had.

But so what? Nothing to be done about it, except seeing how perseverance can sometimes lead to an ambiguous result?

And when does perseverance become "pig-headed?"

On Love: (Age 12+)

When childhood ended and adolescence began in my life, at about 12 years of age, I began to experience a peculiar kind of attraction towards young boys and later men, of about my own age, which led to some experimentation with it as I grew into adolescence. I believe this may be a not uncommon experience among boys at that age. The attraction consisted of a desire to be in the company of one such as I, with whom I could spend time, have joint experiences, explore new fields, develop a deep friendship and in a sense, share my life with. This unformed, but intense desire continued and developed in my adolescence. I did not comprehend, analyze, or try to forget that desire. It was strong. One distinguishing feature of it was that the attraction developed towards men who were basically the opposite of what I was. If I had blond hair, brown eyes and white skin, they had to have the opposite: brown or black hair, blue eyes, and tanned skin, and so forth. The basis for that desire was that I considered myself to be unattractive or incomplete, and desired to have an idealized image of myself as somebody to love

Many years later, in my forties, I began to understand that desire and put it in place in my development. I reached the conclusion that what in fact I had experienced was, in psychological terms, the action of having fallen in love with an idealized image of <u>myself!</u> A specific form of narcissism, posing as a self-deprecating dislike of oneself. This had led to a number of failed encounters with other men, and the end of several meaningful friendships and relationships, because of course they could not live up to my unreal expectations. How could they?I was expecting them to be an idealized, fictional version of myselfWhen I finally realized the real nature of my false expectations, and then abandoned them, it greatly increased my enjoyment of my subsequent life, when I left all of this mental baggage behind and began to see other people in their true light, and not according to my fancies. It was a significant beneficial change in my life thereafter.

My Other Name

When I was a member of a Boy Scout group in my early youth, (about age 12) they had a tradition of the leaders and our other companions giving each one of us a specific name, which usually consisted of an animal's name. accompanied by a qualifying adjective.

The name I was given was "Leopardo Taciturno" in Spanish. or "Taciturn Leopard". In retrospect, I realized that the "alternate" name was extremely appropriate, because I realized that I always liked cats, lions, cheetahs, bob cats and the rest of the cat family, and their quiet but fierce, independent ways, and also because at that time and after that, I was quite taciturn, which is defined by the dictionary as "habitually silent or reserved; disinclined to conversation"

Being "taciturn" was, in my case, not only an accurate description of my usual behavior in company, but also a deliberate defense tactic in my armory. Being a young boy and beginning to be faced for the first time with life's complexities, I think after the very initial period of wonder and enchantment, many boys in my position experience confusion in life, complicated with the sudden irruption of other people's opinions, judgement, and preferences. It is an uncomfortable irruption, and the usual defense techniques are either surrender and submission, or else building up a wall against the world, and decidedly ignoring any easy communication with it, or other words, becoming "taciturn". The latter maneuver, then, I consider very healthy and effective, as long as it is essentially discontinued at a later time in life, because it allows a period of time in which the individual personality can develop, determining which qualities and aptitudes it chooses to follow in later life, without the interference of excessive extraneous inputs.

GREGORY RABASSA

"I am a native of a period made up of three decades. These are the years when a person becomes himself. The years before were a germination, those following the melting icing on an already baked cake. My formation took shape in the thirties, the forties, and the fifties, a fearsome triad of decades which did indeed call for the brontosaurian efforts at survival and sanity".

TRIPS TO EUROPE

When I was about 15 years old, I was lucky to be selected to join a group of about 10 Cuban Boy Scouts to attend a big international meeting of many thousands of boys from all over the world held in Moisson, France in the summer of 1947. We were all camping out in tents in a vast valley in the middle of Northern France.

We travelled to Europe from Cuba by boat to Miami, by train to Washington and New York, and then by a Polish cargo steamer from New York to Cannes, and then by road to Northern France. The Polish boat, the M.S. Sobieski was just a plain old cargo ship with no luxuries, and the passengers were mostly desolate Europeans, returning to Europe after the war to visit relatives or to return permanently, including a large group of Jews who had fled Europe from the war and Hitler's persecutions. The signs aboard ship were of course all in Polish, and I remember a special one "Alarmowa Pozarowa Rosbif" which struck us as peculiar, especially the "roast beef": part, because we never could figure out what it really meant.

The return trip was especially interesting, because we visited Paris and its sights, Switzerland and did some alpine climbing, Milan and its Duomo and Opera House, Spain, Biarritz, and finally Cannes again, where we boarded the ship back to New York. During the international gathering, our camp was personally visited by the Prince of Lichtenstein and some representatives of British royalty, to whom we paid our due respects.

A number of peculiar incidents happened during that trip, which in any case was extremely beneficial to me, because it gave my young eyes the experience of seeing a vast territory all around Northern and Southern Europe, and to meet a varied collection of people; an experience not normally available to a teenager. At that time, just a couple of years after the end of the World War, most of Europe was still suffering from scarcity in many things, including food. As we travelled North in France, we were graciously along the way, lodged with families of other local scouts, and we found that their food was strictly rationed. We were offered only a very sparse menu where we stayed, because many foods were simply unavailable. We encountered similar scarcities in most of the places we visited, except maybe in Switzerland, which was not involved in the war. It was quite an evident fact to us what terrible price Europe had to pay as a consequence of the war, especially the countries that were invaded.

Years later, on one of my vacations from work, I took another trip to Europe, this time on the Queen Mary, which was still running transatlantic voyages, and I could enjoy myself in the luxury of a post-war liner trip, as well as noting the changes for the better that I noticed in Europe, which by then had recovered from a lot of the war damage and bombings. That was also a much more enjoyable trip aboard the liner, because I met several very pleasant and attractive girls my age aboard it, and we hit it off very well during the trip.

AN ADOLESCENT FRIEND AND BUDDY: (1947).- (AGE 15)

I had a close buddy when I was about 15-17 years old. His name was Arcadio, and he was a year older than I, and was somewhat lean, had a wide forehead and blond hair, fine features, and was always ready to laugh. He was not the athletic type that exhibits himself on beaches, but neither was he weak or sickly, or avoided wearing bathing suits. He loved to walk along the countryside, and could swim in style. What stood out in his character were a stupendous imagination and an intelligence quite superior to that of our classmates. I had always been rather closed to others in my habits and thoughts, so I was impressed with his mental out-going quickness. Our differences in character were overcome by the similarity of our tastes and preferences.

At that time I was also very attracted to his sister, which contributed to my frequent visits and frequent outings with him.

We spent many weekends in his family's beach home, where we could give free rein to our desire to explore and discover things, and as a result of this, I believe that in less than three years, we had visited every path, cave lagoon or forest existed within 4 0r 5 miles from that house. On Sundays, we used to go by a certain path known only to us, following a river, to a cave where we unearthed bones presumably belonging to ancient Indians who had once lived there centuries ago.

Arcadio was my friend, the hero that every boy needs to imitate and copy. It was due to our friendship that we jointly acquired the love of books and reading, as well as independence in thinking, loves of science and of nature, the desire to learn, ideas that possible I carried unconsciously before, but were animated and underlined in his company. Unfortunately his well-to-do parents did not quite understand him or particularly encourage him, so Arcadio learned to become independent very early in life and they gave him a free hand to do so. I well remember the many adventures that we participated in together, and I believe it was one of the happiest periods of my adolescence. His precocious desire to know, combined with my selectivity and cooperation lead us to buy books on numerology, prisms, telescopes, maps, navigation charts, camping and camping equipment, geology, astronomy, and many other similar subjects, then spending hours reading and discussing them together. Our various andmultiple investigations led us to visit bookstores, vendors of chemical products and lab equipment, Chinese-owned shops, museums, native dances, taxidermy, and many such others.

It was thus how a couple of small but well-varied libraries (his and mine) began to take shape, which I have continued to keep and enlarge throughout my whole life, even to this day. As all of aware boys, we had a strong desire for adventure an exploration. Our passion for the sea and our wish to navigate, led us into fishing underwater, so we bought goggles and spears and went spear-fishing many times. Ione of these explorations led us to a property which had a very deep, abandoned water well. We descended down to the very bottom, scaling down the vertical wall with the aid of a rope, found the well was dry, and had a cave at the bottom, which we preceded to explore. We had some difficulty in climbing back the 100 feet or so to the surface, but we made it safely.

Another time, we decided to climb up a vertical rock wall in a nearby hill. He had already reached the top and I followed behind him, but slipped as I nearly reached the top and fell a good 10 feet downhill, until I was able to grasp and hold on to a rock sticking out of the wall. It was difficult to slowly climb back up again and reach the top. It was one of the few times I saw my friend blanched in his face from the fear of seeing me fall.

Our friendship came to a temporary end when I went to college for several years, although it renewed upon my return, but we were both at a different stage in our lives, and the warmth that characterized our early friendship was no longer there. We remained in occasional contact, until some years later I sadly found out that he had passed away.

Early friendships like the one we had can have a very large positive influence in an adolescent: they can determine the course of lives, the election of a profession, our philosophy in life, and our choices we make. I am very happy to have had Arcadio in my life.

Source Unknown.- (1944)-(Age 16)

"A solitary, unused to speaking what he sees and feels, has mental experiences which are at once more intense and less articulate than those of a gregarious man. They are sluggish, yet more wayward and never without a melancholy tinge, sights and impressions which others brush aside with a glance, a light comment, a smile, occupy him more than their due, they sink silently in, they take on meaning, they become experience, emotion, adventure. Solitude gives birth to the original in us, to beauty, infamous or perilous— to poetry, but also it gives birth to the opposite: to the perverse, the illicit, the absurd."

A Conclusion tentatively reached.- (1949)-(Age 17)

"A man cannot expect to receive both friendship and respect"
(It has to be one or the other)

Maya and Inca

I was fortunate that my parents encouraged me in most any project I wanted to undertake as a teenager, and even going as far as agreeing to pay for some of them. One of these, was when I was about fifteen years old, I came across some written material about the Mayans in Mexico and Central America. The subject fascinated me and I proposed to take a trip alone to the Mayan country in Mexico and explore the ruins of their ancient cities. My parents agreed to cover the cost and I took off fo about a month in my quest, visiting a number of ruined cities and their majestic buildings while reading all I could about them. As I have mentioned before, at fifteen

I looked much older, perhaps 21 and beyond, so it was no surprise to anyone seeing a young man travelling alone as a tourist. The trip was fascinating, and I became very knowledgeable about the life of the ancient Mayans, although I also found out how barbaric and cruel they had been, offering frequent human sacrifices to their gods, killing some of their young men and women by slitting thir throats in specially constructed altars. This cooled my enthusiasm, but the history of those peoples remained with me and taught me something about human nature.

Later on in life, I had a similar opportunity while visiting the ancient Inca sites in Peru and Ecuador. They were equally fascinating as I learned about their customs, traditions, and behavior and their decadence and eventual collapse of their empire when the Spaniards arrived from the north. *Sic transit….etc etc.*

In Peru, native tribes from the time of the Incas are still very much alive and functioning, often in wild areas of the jungle, very little influenced by Western civilization, speaking their own language, and with relatively very little contact outside their own territories. I had the unusual opportunity to visit some of them and my memories are very special. With some I participated in ceremonies led by the native shamans, and these include hallucinatory experiences never to be forgotten. These people live in the middle of the open jungle, totally dependent on it for food, support and cover, and possess none of the conveniences associated with urban life. It is amazing how they have been able to sustain themselves over centuries, living a life not too different from the one they lived at the time of the Conquest. Our world still has these remnants of past times and epochs in faraway places, that seem not to have affected by the passage of time.

The Mathematics Professor.- A short story

It has been sometimes said that the three turning points in a man's life come when he attains puberty, when he chooses a career and when he chooses a wife. Dan was precisely undergoing his second one. The tremendous doubts, the healthy certainty of the approaching future, the driving ambition to succeed, were all there, intensified further by that virulent form of idealism present in a young man of 18 with supreme confidence in his abilities and an egotistical concern about himself so often manifest in such a one.

Perhaps the most evident feeling at that time in his life was a nonconformist's disagreement with life around him, a burning desire to change and improve, to modify and alter the face of the earth, and to erase the blemishes too apparent in the world and in humanity, with a zeal which was personal and inexperienced, and therefore so unpromising as to underestimate the weight of all the age-old causes of the foul-smelling spots, and to throw out the window any objection or barrier placed in the way of this renovating impulse; his judgement was that these objections were too banal or too foolish to waste time over them with his young and burning mind.

Dan had all these common qualities as well as an additional half-formulated wish to associate himself with such adults in whom he could find an echo of these sentiments, those he could consider as models to follow in his still developing personality. When he started college, the apparition of Professor Stillford as Dan's mathematics professor seemed to be evidence of one of these superior models to follow in his own life, not limited strictly to mathematics per se, but to life as a whole. It became a variation of infantile hero-worship. Stillford had the appearance and characteristics which could be imagined proper to a mathematics professor; he seemed absorbed by the intricacies of the science of numbers, the science of sciences as they call it. He had obtained his Doctor's degree in mathematics at a well-known university, followed by a stint in government work m statistics and mathematical research, and finally ended in his job at a distinguished engineering school where Dan was studying. He was a kind, accessible man and had won the respect of his associates and students for many years. Yet Stillford was always clothed in what might be called a cloak of reserve. He seemed to maintain himself aloof from his fellow professors and there was definitely something about him which insisted on being respected. He had the fame of being the best teacher in the department, a fact which led to ardent discussions among students on which one was indeed the best. Those student circles vanished in a puff of smoke as soon as Stillford came into the room with that peculiar gait of his, and a good-smelling pipe aristocratically he inserted between his teeth.

In the first day of class, Dan immediately liked Stillford, and as the days went by, his admiration of the imposing college professor grew in size and importance. Stillford remained behind his usual reserve although he occasionally smiled and joked in class.

Dan wondered if the professor liked him as a student, but he wasn't sure.

Stillford became to Dan the impersonation of a number of ideals he had unconsciously developed since his earliest youth, ideals of pride and honor, of efficiency and wisdom, and so many others he could not exactly define or even suspect their presence. The ideals of what an adult man should be: intelligent, personable, friendly, capable, functional, well-versed in his specialty or profession, etc. Those ideals have been important in my subsequent life.

This leads me to consider how important it is in the development of a young man to have examples or models to follow early on in life, and what a waste exists in cases where a young man DOES NOT have such examples to imitate, as happens in many cases. The end result of such absence is in the twisted, unhappy, miserable lives of some adult men, often ending in delinquency, dysfunctionality, or just plain unhappiness, when they have not been lucky enough to come across good examples of mature manhood in their family or among friends and acquaintances.

A BIG SIGNPOST. - William B. Yeats-(1952)-(Age 19)

When I went to college (1949-1953), midway, aged about 19, I took a course in modern poetry, given by another exceptionally gifted and intelligent professor, who thankfully introduced me to the best of modern poetry. I am very grateful to him, because some of the poetry in the course clearly spelled out in attractive language some of the same problems and issues I was actually experiencing in my own life. So it was a great teaching for me to realize that famous poets and thinkers had grappled with the same subjects I was facing. One of those poems was a William Butler Yeats poem, which made a very big impressions on me, and I tried thereafter to put in practice in my own life, the thoughts expressed in his poem: :

"A Dialogue of Self and Soul":

"I am content to follow to its source
every event in action or in thought
measure the lot, forgive myself the lot!
When such as I cast out remorse
so great a sweetness flows into the breast
we must laugh and we must sing
we are blest by everything
everything we look upon is blessed".

III

EXPERIMENTATION
(1952 -1972)-(Age 20-40)

Whatever I took a trip to Spain and visited Castile, I passed a location in the country where blindfolded, yoked and harnessed horses tied to a rig of poles, were going slowly around and around a well to get its water out with a system of pulleys. There was no one around watching them or controlling them. The animals were just endlessly going around, period. What a dismal picture! As if no one cared about them, and they were just mechanically moving without any understanding of they were doing or why, with blind acceptance of their fate, and having no choice in the matter. I resolved then and there, never to allow myself to be put in any similar position.

THE ROMAN BATHS

On a vacation trip to Rome, I visited the ancient ruins of Roman baths, extant from over 2000 years ago, and in passing one of the walls, I saw some of the graffiti inscribed there on what was supposed to have been an ancient brothel from such a long time ago. It had a picture of a big phallus and testicles and it read: "HIC HABIT FELICITAS", or "Here dwells happiness".

CAVE EXPLORATION

When I was living in Cuba, I got interested in the exploration of natural caves and caverns. It was a natural interest, because Cuba is largely a limestone island with plentiful running water along its surface, ideal conditions for the formation of natural caverns, and there were many of them along the whole island. These were not small openings into the ground but very large—some even grandiose constructions, some with rivers flowing through their interior, with multitudes of bats living inside their openings, and with occasional pools and underground springs. I was fascinated by them and explored many of them, usually with similarly oriented friends. In fact we formed the Cuban Speleological Society to conduct expeditions to caves and present talks and conferences about that subject. One of our colleagues there was Antonio Nunez Jimenez who was an intelligent and versatile cave-explorer. He, later on, after the revolution, first became a close collaborator of Fidel Castro, later to be labelled a counter-revolutionary and dismissed by the Castro regime. But my experience with him was before all that, I remember him as a good friend and intelligent partner in cave exploring. Together, we wrote an article published in one of the local popular magazines, covering the exploration of the very little known caverns of Santo Tomas in Pinar del Rio, Cuba, which consisted of a big system of connected caves, with a river going through them opening into an enclosed valley and then proceeding through the other side of the valley into yet another mountain. It was wondrous sight and an incredibly natural one. Several years later, after I had moved to and settled in New York and became a U.S. citizen, I suddenly received a telephone call from someone in an agency of the U.S government mentioning that they had read my published articles on Cuban caves, and they wished to interview me personally to ask me some questions about that subject. It was at the time of close Soviet cooperation with Fidel Castro, and the U.S. government people suspected that some missile silos were being installed in Cuba, possibly in the very large Cuban caves, to conceal them from view. After confirming to my satisfaction that they were in fact legitimate, I naturally agreed to meet with them and help them in any way I could so we met for quite a long time in New York, during which I passed on to them all of the information I had on Cuban caves. They graciously thanked me for that, and it was interesting because later on I learned from others that apparently the caves were in fact being used by Castro people at least to store ammunition, and perhaps to conceal some silos as well.

SPEAR FISHING

Another activity I was drawn to, was the sport of spear fishing, Those were the days before oxygen tanks and breathing apparatus were available to breathe under water, so we used only face masks to partly cover our face, which meant you could only dive for few feet beneath the surface before you had to surface again to take a breath. Even so, spearfishing affords a view into a marvelous world of color among tropical coral growths, crystalline waters, and varied underwater vegetation.

It is a world not to be missed. I am very glad I did not miss it, although today I would not wish to contribute to the depletion of marine fauna by going fishing in it. In the tropical waters we fished, we often saw sharks lurking around the reefs, but we avoided them whenever possible, and never suffered a direct attack from them. Apart from being a physically demanding sport, the reward of seeing the incredible colors, and teeming life in the reefs, more than balances out whatever inconvenience is attached to it.

Mountain Climbing

Mountains of any type have always had a special appeal to me and climbing them has always been a pleasure, even when I was a young boy. As a teenager I climbed many hills and mountains, some with my friend Arcadio.

Later on I heard about a mountain-climbing training course which was being offered in the Swiss Alps, no less. I signed up for it as fast as I could and took off for Switzerland for a couple of weeks. The course was being offered in a small village in the very middle of the Swiss Alps, and a group of fifteen or so of us was led by two experienced middle aged guides, who were extremely capable, kind, and careful. We could not have had better leaders. During the course, we climbed a series of peaks in the neighborhood, some while all of us were tied with ropes for safety. The experience was exhilarating and wonderful. The sights were magnificent and the overall program could not have been more satisfying, even though at some points I was afraid I would fall from my perch, into the void many hundreds of feet below me; but these were groundless fears, and all went well. I relished the experience and still have photographs of the more perilous passages.

Cooking

During my boyhood, my mother was not a good cook and did not particularly like cooking. She also did not have good education in proper meals, so I grew up rather fussy about meals and not wanting to eat many foods. Meals were prepared for our large family by a live-in cook.

That began to change during my late teens, when I discovered and began to frequent good restaurants, only to discover the gastronomic pleasures available from enjoying delicious foods. This led to a major interest in food on my part, as I began to experiment with cooking meals myself and discovering what went into them and how to prepare them. It became an interesting hobby and I began to delight in cooking foods for invited friends. One of my guides at that point was a book in Spanish called "Cocina al Minuto",(Cooking by the Minute) by Nitza Villapol and Martha Martinez, which I still have, a wonderful collection of Cuban recipes. Cuban cuisine is an interesting and very tasty mixture of Spanish and Caribbean recipes.

This the led to my taking training courses in food preparation, some spearheaded by the well-known personality of Julia Child, but it didn't stop there. I went on to take a cooking seminar in Paris, following the lineaments laid down by the celebrated gastronome Claude Terrail, cuisine chef of the internationally famous Paris restaurant : "La Tour D'Argent". He also wrote a book called "Tour D'Argent" which I used as one of my 'bibles' in experimenting with cooking. I continued to buy books on gastronomy and cooking for many years, until I was the proud possessor of a substantial library on the subject.

As a natural consequence of this absorbing interest, I began to invite friends and acquaintances for frequent dinners at home in which I tried to excel in the refinement of cooking. I believe this was not only welcomed by my friends, but even more so by me, because it afforded a convenient and pleasant way to stay connected with friends, enjoy their company, and not let friendships cool with the passage of time. I look back on those years of good cooking, full of good memories and good company.

BOTANY

Partly as a result of my acquaintance with an adult friend that was very interested in plants and botany, I acquired an interest in it myself. We had a sizable garden at home and I was attracted to the outdoors, so a connection with plants and their lore was a natural result. I began to eagerly read about them and learn not only their common names, but their Latin names as well. After that, the next step was to begin to collect plant leaves and flowers, putting them on a plant press, and attaching information about their identification, growth, properties, and uses, and binding them in a series of books which I have kept over the years and still have, referring to them often. It can be a fascinating hobby. The variety and range of the plant world is enormous and humanity depends so much on it for food and medicinal properties, that the search is endless. It is tinged with beauty as well, since so many plants produce perfumed and exotic flowers. It has been very satisfying to me to plant a seed or a bulb or a small plant, to care for it, and to see it grow to its full size and bloom.

A LETTER TO BILL—(FROM ANTHONY).- A SHORT STORY

"Dear Bill:

It is now evening and I am sitting in the terrace of this new house I have, so quiet and pleasant. It is bitter cold outside, which is something very unusual for our climate, as you know, but again, it has been an unusual year in so many ways. As I have sat here, listening to some music, I've thought aimlessly of the last few months, the last few years, and in doing so to the years we spent together at college. As I look back upon them, so close and recent in time, and yet so far in life—in my life, which has since been a search for something hidden,............ I realize I was a lucky man.

It was a set of coincidences, or a set of probabilities, which brought us together in what was an unusual and original association—a partnership of a type which you well know had qualities of the extravagant and also of the serious. I realize it now and I am thankful to fate or to whatever you choose to call it, for permitting such a set of circumstances to happen which allowed us to come together. It was a peculiar period of our lives. You never suspected the intensity with which I felt these things—and now I look back upon them with a feeling of illusion and phantasy—the things I grew to associate with your presence and your being: the uncontrolled boyishness, the love of life, the quick sharp turn, the happiness, the unconcern, and at the same time the occasional tortured, sad reaction, the undefined melancholy, the very haze of an undefined desire, of an uncomprehended wish— the strength and confidence you had, and at the same time, the veins of weakness, the soft spots. Perhaps you were never aware of these things, you never looked.

As I remember, all these things: the unconcern, the preoccupation, the understanding you had of things, and the way we felt towards one another as friends, ranging from the unhindered and total understanding, to impatient exasperation. As I look back, often longing for the times, places, the associations, it feels as if two substances were being mixed so intimately, you and I, that it was no longer possible to separate them. I began to feel this way gradually—a hundred different situations led me to it piece by piece: the chill air of a September morning walking about in the Massachusetts' woods, a quick weekend in New York, with the rounds of girls, drinks, places, watching you in your first airplane ride; and also the confused, sad days. In a way, you became for me a symbol of youth, free, careless and clean.

Later on in my life, there were long periods during which we had little or no contact, and still later it so happened that we renewed our friendship, now modified and much improved by our maturity and the passage of time. I look back upon it with a healing smile and welcome feeling, and forward to a period of renewed and close friendship.

Anthony

THE TALES OF HOFFMANN

A couple of years before In graduated from college, I happened to see a movie, "The Tales of Hoffmann" produced in 1951 by Michael Powell and Emeric Pressburger, which was a visual interpretation of the opera by Jacques Offenbach, essentially in the form of a ballet, with well-known artists as interpreters of the key roles, transporting the audience into a world of theatricality and effortless magic, with music conducted by Sir Thomas Beecham. The ballet is an adaptation of three stories in which the poet Hoffmann reminisces about the three unattainable beauties who broke his heart, but inspired his art. The three are simply different facets of the same person, his undying love. Offenbach's music is tender, gracious and extremely appealing.

The first one is acted by the great ballerina Moira Shearer, the second by the incredibly beautiful Parisian dance Ludmilla Tcherina, and the third by the singer Ann Ayars. The second act with Ludmila Tcherina was especially touching to me because it represented a very beautiful woman being rowed along the lagoons of Venice, as she sings the famous "Barcarolle". She is approached by Hoffmann, who is overcome by her attraction and begs her for her love, only to repudiated coolly and definitely.

The movie created a very large impression on me, because at my young age I was uncertain about love and its implications, and the sadness of Hoffmann's regrets, which echoed some of my own feelings regarding close connections with other human beings. The lovely movie raised again my uncertain feelings about love and how to satisfy it. It also definitely touched the ambiguous situation of someone finding himself loving a real person, without realizing that the person is just representing something else, an image, inside himself, without awareness of doing so, a situation that seemed very familiar to me; in other words, loving an image, but not the real person. Such is the impression she made on me, that I still have a copy of Tcherina in my study. I bought a copy of the movie and have seen it again several times in subsequent years.

A REGRETTABLE ACTION.-(1965).-(AGE 33)

"I said a hurting word and you cringed. Your face took on a slight twist of utter humiliation and misery, you laughed with the laugh of those who are about to cry, and you remained silent, and just by that I felt miserable in having hurt you. You whom I have put in a pedestal higher than you can imagine; it made me feel so wretched that I called myself a fool, a thousand times fool to hurt what I most prized, to mar the perfection of a human face with that most damnable of insults: humiliation".

"To hear you feel for me with that expressive look in your eyes, in a room full of people, to hear you laugh and talk aloud to attract my attention, to notice the affected manner you use to make yourself interesting to me. I wonder: will you always be like this?"

I mention the above as a "regrettable" action but I must quickly add that although it certainly was regrettable at the time it happened, I have a much different view of regrets now, of regrets of any kind, and I believe that regrets are useless wastes of energy and lead nowhere. Why? Because the past is past and there is nothing one can do to change it. It is better to accept what happened, to realize one is a human being, and therefore apt to make mistakes, and to live in the present without being burdened by regrets from the past, and not repeating the actions that caused them.

Sex should be experienced with passionate energy, without the need for conquest or possession.

To realize our higher self, to be all we can, to grow to our full potential in awareness. To choose always the 'highest choice', not necessarily what is most convenient, or most profitable, or acceptable to others.

A Dream

I make a phone call to a friend and get an answering machine which says: "This is not an <u>answering</u> machine. This is a <u>questioning</u> machine, and here are two questions for you to answer right now: *Who exactly are you? What is it you truly want in your life?* At the sound of the tone, please record your feeble explanations. Speak clearly, pronounce every syllable, and do not mumble".

There have been thousands of people over many centuries who have tried to answer those very questions about their lives. I wonder: can I answer them myself?

A Terminated Relationship-(Dec. 18, 1966)-(Age 34)

It is a cool, clear Sunday afternoon in New York, and you have been away for a long time in endless invitations, with people you don't really care about. Caged in the box of your indifference, I go out walking, and walk first through the Drive, where children, dogs and old men are catching the sun in the quiet park. There in Central Park, where I am caught by the sunlit sparkle of blond hair of a young cyclist; past the lake and the walks, past the dogs and the stalks, on to the East. As I pass the museum, a twinge of nostalgia. A few blocks later, all of 81st street drowns me in a flood of memory. The places, the times, the friends, the ecstasy.......... and the unhappiness we felt together in that neighborhood. Your spirit and your memory fills every corner, so recently and yet so far in time, like a box put away in remembrance, but not yet remembered. I pass by, my pain increases, the pain of having, yet, not having. As I reach the East River, the pain has become sharp and straight, like a razor that cuts without showing the blade, and I realize that my pain is my need of you. My body and my mind are permeated with you. I think of you wherever I hurt and wonder how deep you will cut and if you realize how deep you can cut.

A Story

They were both in their early twenties, full of desire and lacking experience, Keith and Margie. At that age they both wanted to feel life vibrating through them in full force, and did not concern ourselves too much with possible results or future consequences. The drive was to experience, experience......... experience. Part of it was based on the realization that they had so little of it yet, at that age, and everybody else seemed to have so much more. They were running to catch up with the crowd. They met at a party in a friend's house and after some conversation, made a date for a few days later, and the destination was to be an evening in a local very popular nightclub, which offered a spectacular show, served food and drinks and was patronized by the upper elements in town. That went well, and it was followed by subsequent meetings in similar locales and in common friends' homes. As usual, invariably the question of sex came up in the growing relationship. By that time Keith had had sexual experiences with several women and enjoyed them, but it became apparent that Margie was still very much a virgin. That presented a problem which was soon overcome by her curiosity and his persistence, so the couple ended up one night, after a night club visit, in one of the local motels, where Margie promptly was bedded and lost her virginity with resultant alarms and pleasure to both partners.

All went well for several days, except one day Keith received an imperious call from Margie's mother, asking him to come visit their house as soon as possible. That spelled trouble, but there was no way for him to avoid it. Upon entering the house, he was met by a serious and upset mother, as well as a lawyer father, and a distraught Margie, whereupon the mother promptly said that they were aware of the situation and demanded that Keith marry their daughter right away. After a long silence during which he quickly considered possible replies, he answered that he had just started his first job, which although promising, had not yet afforded him the opportunity to accumulate any savings and was therefore in no position financially to support himself and a spouse, and that marrying now would drive them both to poverty, also mentioning that the sex they had was fully consensual and that he had not forced it on Margie at all, which was the truth. This led to an impasse, after which he gently said goodbye and quietly left the house. The friendship and contact between him and Margie did not continue, after that, although they sometimes saw each other in the circles they frequented. She subsequently married a common friend, and presumably led a happy married life thereafter.

On Corporate Management

It has become fashionable in certain quarters of society, to criticize the behavior of corporations, describing them as money-grabbing entities with no respect for ethics or social responsibilities, interested only in making lucrative profits. My personal experiences as an employee and executive in several major American corporations do not support this view, that I consider an irresponsible opinion from some outside critics who are expounding upon what they are not familiar with. Their view may be true in some exceptional cases, because there are always thieves in the field, but major USA corporations are run for profit, yes, but honestly serving a public that is gladly willing to pay for the products or services offered by those companies, which would not exist without the enterprise, dedication, and hard work put on by them to develop those products.

In the middle period of my life, I devoted it to building up my career and increasing my salary and responsibility by gradually aspiring and reaching ever higher levels of management. I first started out as a Chemical Engineer in a big New York company with worldwide operations. They hired me to spearhead as a chemical project engineer, the transfer of a large manufacturing plant from one old and unsuitable location, to a new, efficient one. After a few years with them, during which I performed similar project engineering assignments, I realized that my future promised nothing but more of the same. While I enjoyed the performance and was good at it, I was looking forward to more general management experience and higher compensation, so I resigned my position to accept a job in international management, where my language proficiency in English, Spanish, French and Italian could be put to use. In that new job, I was put in charge of an international division with 6 overseas subsidiaries, in the business of making and selling agricultural product and machinery. This was a wonderful opportunity for me because it increased the scope of my practice, gave me increased responsivity, higher salary, and the opportunity to deal in international business. That led to temporarily living for several years in Spain, Italy Greece, France, England, and Israel, while retaining my home in New York. It multiplied my management experience, and during that time I came across a series of what one could call management 'principles' or practices, borrowed from management conferences or articles, which I adopted as my own. They did much to propel my career, and I not only tried to implement them, but also teach managers under me in thie use and application. Here is a simplified list of them:

1. "The best way to play games: don't".
2. "Work for the person you work for".
3. "Old Navy saying: Men do what is inspected, not what is expected".
4. "People pay a high price when they make decisions that are incompatible with each other".
5. "Never make a decision on anything until you have to. When you have to, make the decision immediately".
6. "Managers must manage: this means taking action to achieve a desired result. Inactivity, postponement, procrastination, complaining,----------these are all non-actions and non- management".
7. Some famous nonsense:
   a) "it isn't what you do that counts, it's how you do it". Sheer poppycock. What counts is results. You're in the game to win, not to be a good loser".
   b) "Keep up the good work". What work? Please specify or else I won't understand what you're referring to.
   c) "Learn from your mistakes". Another turkey. You can't learn from your mistakes because all they can teach you is how to make more good mistakes. How about learning from your successes?
   d) "Experience is the best teacher". What experience? You may have been doing the same wrong thing for 10 years. Experience is valuable only when it is understood and analyzed.
   e) "This is the way we do things around here". Well, maybe you should stop that and do them a different way. Change is the only constant.
   f) A thought: turnover is bad enough. what's worse is that we have lost so many people that are still with us.

"His power consists of this: he knows what he wants, at any special moment, in a more precise form than any one of us does."

Ultimately, the efficient and functioning executive is one who is able to make choices and evaluate the risk to himself and to his ambition, with an adult acceptance of the fact that he cannot have his cake and eat it too. One cannot climb a mountain, however, without the risk of falling off. Any executive, who has made it to the top, has lived intimately with this very image. Whether at the summit he finds himself above the clouds, confronted by a breath-taking panorama of the world below him, or in a precarious, windy niche, or with yet another mountain on his path, depends not so much in what mountain he climbed, as on who is and how he got there. If he can adapt happily to his accomplishment, he will reap all of the rewards that his long years of struggle sowed. But if it overwhelms him, and true to his character he plunges, brave and solitary into a lonelier struggle than any he has yet attempted, it is possible that ultimately success may not seem worth the price he has paid.

"Success in any business is seldom a 'flash in the pan'. It comes about only when you do things <u>right</u>, time and <u>again</u>. If it sounds a little boring......sorry, if you want excitement, become an actor and starve."

An Incredibly Useful Management Tool,-

When I was working for Procter and Gamble, I learned about a very useful tool that the company used with all of their supervisors: they required all of their supervisors to write a weekly report to their boss or bosses. The weekly report was supposed to be only one or two pages long (rarely more) and it had to contain the following sections in that order:

1.-Subject, 2.-Conclusions,
3.-Recommendations, 4.-Discussion

The subject was expected to be anything that you had noted about the operation you were supervising that could be improved, modified, re-arranged or in any way changed for the better, and that of course included what actions you had taken to implement your recommendations. It could refer to layout, organization, methods, reporting, change in operation or anything that would in fact improve the area you were supervising.

It was simply a superb method of emphasizing the function of any supervisor to improve his operation by remaining alert to anything that would improve its efficiency, save costs, improve morale, or in any way make the process better. The results were astonishing because it pointed any supervisors attention to what needed to be improved, and as a result it produced constant change for the better. It is a system that I think should be implemented in any organization, because it focuses attention in the right places, and the positive results are amazing.

———————————⊙———————————

WHAT IT TAKES.- A SHORT STORY

What does it take to lead a happy, rewarding and successful life? The right answer is actually quite complex. It is not reducible to a few simple maxims, and can vary significantly between individuals depending on their background, history, family relationships, and a palette of other factors not easily generalized.

Charlie Simms was a successful manager who had come up through the ranks of his company, originally starting out with a technical degree, and gradually expanding his prowess in dealing with all kinds of problems in ramming a division of a large company manufacturing and marketing specialized types of equipment used in agriculture. His good record and experience led the management of his employer to transfer him to a distant city where the company's headquarters were located, with a substantial promotion and increase of compensation for him.

He was asked by management to suggest a replacement to take over his job as general manager, from the ranks of his own division. He therefore considered the managers reporting to him and selected a relatively young man, Lon Hisham, who was in charge of quality control of the division and had also come up through the ranks due to his intelligence, vigor, and easy way of relating with his co-workers, and passed Lon's name up to headquarters, which then proceeded to appoint Lon as Charlie's replacement as General Manager. At the time, Lon was married and had two young children.

After a short period of training Lon, Charlie then moved to the headquarters city and had no further connection or responsibility for his former division, having then been assigned to a completely different operation.

Everything seemed to go well for both after the transition; but suddenly, one day, Charlie got a telephone call from Lon, who was overtly crying on the phone, and brokenly attempted to tell Charlie that he had just resigned from his job and the company, and was planning to leave town. When Charlie attempted to find the reasons why he had been led to this abrupt decision, Lon could only half mumble some sentences trying to explain that he just had come to the realization that he was just not capable, in other words incompetent, to perform the job that he had been appointed to, and that his life seemed to have been deprived of any meaning and he saw no way out of this, except to resign. He did not seem to have any plans as to what to do next, or where to go, and promptly hung up. Charlie never heard from Lon again.

What could have happened to Lon? Was it in fact lack of capacity, loss of spirit, domestic family problems, a life crisis?

Was it Charlie's big error in judgement of an employee who seemed to him capable and in fact was not? It is not easy to correctly judge another human being and his capacities. Who knows!

So what did in fact happen? The answer lies in the importance for every human being to develop as early as possible a very well defined sense of personal identity: to know well what he or she is all about, to believe in oneself and the importance of being alive, regardless of the circumstances that affect us, and so to speak to "above it all". This extends to avoidance of hurting any other living being, and to acceptance of responsibility that we have freely entered to, including termination of it when untenable situations demand it. Marriage or close associations with other human beings cannot be allowed to destroy a life if they have become unworkable and have to be ended if necessary, as well as friendships which have gone sour.

Not a simple answer to lead a happy successful life! It takes guts, intelligence and good judgement.

A Lucky Break

After several productive and satisfying years as general manager of the international division in the West Coast of the USA of my employer company, which I have described above, one fine morning I received a call from my boss in our East Coast headquarters, telling me that our whole company had been just acquired by a very large corporation also located in the East. This came as a big surprise, because neither I nor any of my colleagues had known anything about this impending purchase. Naturally we were all concerned about how our new owner would act; would we keep our jobs? Were they a good employer? What changes would come about? No answers were forthcoming right away, so we just took one day at a time and waited for developments.

Sometime thereafter I received a call from the secretary of the Chairman of the Board of the corporation that had acquired us, telling me that he was visiting the different divisions of the company he had just acquired, and that he would be paying a visit of several days to our offices in the West Coast in the coming week, giving me the exact date of his coming. Naturally, I was eagerly looking forward to his visit, wondering how that would affect my future and the future of the operations I headed.

I made suitable preparations, arranging to have my office made ready for him to use during his stay, providing him to use my secretary for any work he might want her to do, and readying our personnel for his visit, as well as making a reservation for him in a suitable nearby hotel.

On the arranged day, this personable, well-dressed and powerful man arrived, and I proceeded to show him around our offices and manufacturing facilities, and also suggested we might visit some of our field sales locations as well as customers. This he readily accepted to do, and took him around these visits, including the office of competitor company which I was hoping we might induce him acquire and make it it a part of our operation. All of these meetings went quite well and after a few days he moved on to other locations, not before thanking me for his welcome.

Two or three weeks later, I received a telephone call from outlining his plan for me to be appointed his "Assistant to the Chairman", effective the following week, which meant I had to physically move my home from California to the East Coast, and take on this vastly increased responsibility, along with the consequent increased salary!. I was overwhelmed by his offer and as much as I regretted having to leave California, it made sense to me to thankfully accept that promotion, which I did.

I found out that he had established a practice to appoint promising young executives as his Assistant for one or two years, and then assign them to other important jobs in one of the divisions of the company. It was an excellent practice, because it provided the company with capable executives trained by him, and also it was a great way to promote managers within the company.

In my new job, I was exposed in a very complete way to the workings of a large corporation from an unequalled position: I had a view from the very top and could not ever have attained the experience I did from any other corporate job. I am very thankful to him for having been given that exceptional opportunity. After some time in that position, he eventually assigned me to manage a large division he had recently acquired, and which I led as President for several years. That experience further matured my capabilities. Eventually, the inevitable happened: he got older and decided to retire.

I knew this was going to be bad news for me, because his replacement had no personal connections to me, and in fact the time came shortly thereafter when I saw no future in my career there, and left the company to head out on my own.

There were a few years left before my usual retirement age, so I purchased several franchises and ran them profitably for a while until they were sold, and then I retired for good. Happily, I had accumulated enough savings by that time so between those and my pension income, I had enough income to live on for the rest of my life.

THE SURPRISING MEANING OF DREAMS.- (1970)- (AGE 38)—DAT AND ACER

Dreams seem to contain ethereal or dramatic stories that often seem to have no connection with our lives. Sometimes they do, and that is the subject of unending psychiatric theories about their importance and their meaning. I have had my share of dreams in my life, but one specially stands out, which is described below:

I dream that I am in a jungle, most probably
in the Amazon, looking for and collecting plants.
I am accompanied by a friend who knows the

location well and is guiding me. Suddenly, we come upon a big warehouse type of building, with lots of books and publications inside stacked in many shelves. I am simply a curious visitor there, not looking for anything special, but I am very interested and consult many of the books and literature stored there. In the course of these researches, we come upon references to presumably a very important chemical called "DAT". I have never come across that word before and ignore where it comes from, and whether it is really an acronym rather than an actual word.

My companion tells me that that word stands for a chemical extracted from a plant, the name of which is "ACER". I have also never heard that word before. He then brings a cut stem of the actual plant which is just a normal plant stem, but seems a little fuzzy or hairy on its bark. I feel as if I had been given important information,.

At that point, I wake up from my dream and right away write down the names "ACER" and "DAT", and go back to sleep.

Next morning, after I wake up, I look up both words in the dictionary and other reference materials. To my complete surprise, I find that "DAT" stands for Diamyl Triptamine, which is a psychoactive chemical having an indole group with two 5-Carbon chains attached to a Nitrogen. It also turns out that "ACER" means a tree or shrub of the Maple family, the Aceraceae. In fact "ACER" means a maple!----and "acerous" or "acerose" means "chaff-like". How did my friend appear in the dream showing a plant cutting, and calling it by the name "ACER" which in effect means a maple a name and meaning which he did not know himself. How did the connection appear in the dream? And what is the connection between "DAT" and a maple? Does the sap of a maple contain "DAT"? I have not yet found the answer to that question.

So putting these apparently meaningless (to me) words together in a dream, inexplicably made a lot of crazy sense. The mind operates in fancy ways!

ON FEAR

"It comes like the wind. Let the wind blow."

Three Sayings I heard and Liked.-

1. It is better to have a plan for your life, or else you become a part of someone else's plan.
2. It is better to explore unknown territory alone, rather than use a map made by tourists.
3. It is better to kill an infant on its cradle, than to nurse un-acted on desires.

Should we be surprised?

We each live within the circle of our own consciousness, blissfully unaware of such chasms as we pass on our way, concerned only with the occurrences, big or small, which dot our own particular landscape. Emotional creatures that we are, we go about our daily plans and projects, assuming that our own decisions will affect the course of our immediate future. Yet how often is that future affected by so many unpredictable currents, by the decisions of others, by the sweeping flow of human events around us in which we play but little parts, by the whims of fate..........even by the mere influence of a moment, a fleeting attitude, an instant of understanding.

Should we be surprised then, when by some unforeseen turn of chance, we glimpse for an instant, a view of other worlds around us? When we intrude upon those worlds of others.......which seem so alien, and yet may be so related to our own mad progress?

Carl Jung: "The psyche has a thousand ways to terminate a life that has become meaningless".

Two betrayals

Earlier in my life, when I was travelling around Europe on a vacation, I stayed in Paris for a while, and there I met a very intelligent and attractive young man, who was a German living in Paris, and having a grand time of it. He knew Paris quite well and as we struck up a friendship, he was kind enough to show me some of the sights of Paris which I would never have known about on my own, especially the night life. The friendship grew over the years and every time I was in Paris I looked him up and had a good time together. Eventually when I was living in California I invited him to come visit me there, and we made some preliminary plans as to time and travel. Shortly after, however he wrote me and said he could not come because he did not have enough money to pay for his trip to the USA. I felt confident enough of his abilities so I offered to pay for his trip, and he could reimburse me later, and then sent him the necessary money to cover his round trip. He kept the money and never came, alleging that he was very busy and could not come. I discontinued any contact with him and never saw him again.

I felt very betrayed, of course.

The second disappointment came from a young man that I employed as a manager in one of the small businesses I was operating after my corporate retirement. He was capable and effective, and we became good personal friends, often playing racquetball together. I enjoyed his company and tried to help him whenever I could, often including in some short trips I took within the area, and often inviting him to dinner at my home. After some years, however, I found out that he had been systematically stealing money from the business he was running for me as manager. I was forced to let him go right away and I have never heard or seen him since.

Two disappointments in judging people, and two important lessons learned about when, and how much, to trust people. They helped me in deciding on these two points thereafter with more wisdom and precaution.

On Indices.- A Letter To Daniel

"Following our preliminary discussion on this subject......and at your request....after much cogitation and elucubration, I have finally settled on my proposals for a chrestomathy of the different indices into which it is appropriate,...nay, necessary infeed...to place different acquaintances one comes up across in normal daily intercourse. These I submit to you below, for proper assimilation and subsequent use.

You may remember that this train of thought was started upon our consideration of the infamous "Index Librorum Prohibitorum", or index of prohibited books, which the flatulent Catholic Church fathers imposed on their compliant congregations, several centuries ago. In other words, you cannot read these books, under penalty of being excommunicated if you do.

For simplicity's sake, I thought that these indices should be condensed to just the three below, but eventually these basic ones could be expanded into several dozen, but that labor I shall l leave to the scribes. At any rate, here they are:

1. INDEX AUREUM.- how could this be called by any other name than the "golden Index", the auriferous index, which would naturally include books written by authors who can call upon us at any time of night or day, for any reason, or for no reason at all, such as just to engage in persiflage or badinage, and whom we would welcome and enjoy at any time. In other words, those who make life enjoyable and worth living. The raison d'etre for having good friends: the best and exquisite reward.

2. INDEX MINIMA LINGUA ET NON SEQUITUR.- This classification would be used for authors who are basically OK, but where the chemistry doesn't really work, and with whom we would be happy to exchange a few pleasantries, without going into the exertions of a more demanding relationship. In other words, the "non sequitur" means that we would not make any effort to follow up.

3. <u>INDEX SCUMBAGUS MUNDI ET JACTATIO NUCIS</u>.- Needless to say, this index would be reserved for the scum bags of the world......all one can do is to throw coconut's at them......i.e. 'jactatio nucis'. In this hopefully restricted classification would be placed those authors who fuck up the world and leave nothing but a trail of smelly, worthless books behind and around them. In other words, we want to have no truck with them. I can think of a couple of them that I have met during my life, one for example being that snake- in the grass charlatan, medicaster, botcher, quack, tooth-puller, and fumbler, Dr K. There are two or three more that I can rmember.

I hope this preliminary outline gets your intellect moving into these delightful areas of exercise, and I am sure I will hear from you on corrections, amplifications, and elaborations of this scheme. Since we are using so much Latin, *DE HOC SATIS*: enough of that!

I read about a conversation between Lady Astor and Winston Churchill that is supposed to have gone as follows:

<u>Lady Astor</u>: "If I were your wife, I would put arsenic in your coffee."

<u>Winston Churchill</u>: "And if I were your husband, madam, I would drink it".

So many times, those people on which I have caused a better impression than one I could live up to, have asked me to tell them that I love them, that now I am beginning to associate the word love with unwanted, artificial feelings. This is why I am surprised when I can freely tell you that I love you...I love you!......without you having asked for it, and with all the intensity and freedom from artificiality that I am able to muster!

I can experience desire, and look for myself in other beings, be surprised to receive familiar echoes, hope for a mirror that will reflect my image, need pleasure and enjoyment, and all of this may appear to be love.

ARISTOTELES, ON THE ELEUSINIAN MYSTERIES

"The participant doesn't have to learn anything. All he has to do is receive impressions and emotions, after making himself worthy, of course, to receive them."

Arsenio

It was late afternoon when I finished packing my suitcase and collecting holiday gear, putting it in the trunk of the car, to set out for a carefree weekend in the distant beach. By the time I left the city and reached the highway, which hugs the warm, blue-green sea for miles eastward, it was already dark. Dusk in the tropics is a peculiar, prolonged moment, when everything seems suspended in time, and motion itself seems paralyzed as in some pagan ritual. Whereas in colder climates the transition from day to night is brisk and uncompromising, in the tropics it shadows of inland trees. I often asked myself where they came from other than the sterile expanse of the unending sea?.

I had worked long and hard that day. One more in the series of similar days, where the factory produced endless cases of the familiar product, with the usual share of problems to be solved, and decisions to be made. This was the lot of my job as a chemical engineer; I could think of worse jobs. At least, here was a process where I could observe the immediate result of my decisions, where things happened because they had to happen, and because it had been planned for them to happen. There was an air of predictability. This particular predictability had the effect of a balm on the young man I was then, one with deep-lying, imprecise doubts about life in general. Perhaps it was this quality of sureness, of the desire for certainty that had induced me to become an engineer. At any rate, I was tired, and looking forward to a weekend of unbridled relaxation in quite different surroundings from the drab steel-grays of the manufacturing plant. As the car surged forward on the unwinding black strip of basalt, I left these thoughts behind, and let my mind wander ahead of me to the life on a sparkling azure beach where I was headed, and the pilgrim group of friends whom I would join.

In the tropics, life is slow, as if the vital processes going on in warm temperatures suddenly agreed to a temporary cease-fire. The city, seen from a distance, was a mirage of pale red images when the last rays of the sun impinged upon the plaster of the far away walls. As the speeding car followed the highway, the sun's disk sank into the all-embracing sea. Blackbirds in rugged flights flew in from the coast to the protective trees inland.

How had I come to know them? How had I opened up my own intimate circle to so different an outer world?

Memories of the past few months came flooding back into my brain, as the cool night air enveloped me. My employment with a big American corporation, the long period of training in the big factory, the gradual acquiring of technical skills; then, finally, the overseas assignment, the trip to Havana, Cuba, the taking over of my job in the local subsidiary, and my adjustment to new faces, new things, new friends.

It had all started a few months back when Marita called me on one sultry afternoon at my office. Her girlish voice sounded peculiarly naïve, when she insisted I join her that evening, in a rehearsal of an amateur theatrical production which some of her friends were staging. It was to be presented some weeks later at a large resort hotel in Varadero Beach, the proceeds going to a local children's orphanage. I was uncertain about accepting the invitation, having visions of bustling do-gooders, and charitable matrons. But Marita's insistence had that persuasive quality of some women who seem never to have developed beyond the stage of demanding adolescence.

My mind was still absorbed by the problems of the past days' work when that evening, we drove up to a great house with extensive gardens, in one of the best residential areas of Havana, where the rehearsal was to take place. As we were shown in by a uniformed butler, I remember being impressed by the large mirrors paneling the walls of the entrance hall, a myriad of our own glassy eyes being reflected back upon us. Marita soon vanished into the large garden where loud music was playing. A large group of people milled about. She soon came back, followed by a young, tall man to whom I was introduced. He was Arsenio, the organizer of the whole affair. I can remember his eyes; they flashed a light of curiosity and interest, as if looking for a new emotion, a varied experience, a different viewpoint. He was mostly silent, but his eyes revealed his vitality.

We went into the garden, where I recognized some acquaintances. I soon found out this was no ordinary group. They were representatives of the richest and best families of the city, known to each other and to the public, aware of their position and fully acknowledging it. Most of them were in their twenties, as I was. They represented the second and third generations of the established society of the island, that elite that derived from the old days of the Spanish upper class, when the island of Cuba was still a Spanish colony before 1900, or from the families which emerged into dominant public life in the independence struggles, or in fortune-creating decades at the beginning of the 20th century.

As we moved about in the garden, I tried to fit into the pattern and soon found myself included in a small group that was rehearsing to dance a Charleston number in a charity show. Itwas supposed to be a full-fledged revival of the flapper age, complete with straw hats and wide-striped coats. Before I knew it, I was practicing Charleston steps with a dozen other people, to the metallic tunes of "Has anybody seen my gal?"

The atmosphere in the whole house was alive, vibrant, with the eagerness of ambitious personalities and excited youth. It was contagious—it made one move with a sense of continuous expectations. An amused smile came to my face, comparing this with the organized pattern of everyday experience at the factory. A big change from manufacturing machinery to Charleston capers!

That first night I was hooked! Drawn gradually into the circle of friends, I found myself being well-accepted, perhaps partly on account of my native reticence, which was in direct contrast with the usual open manner of the group. I was soon closely identified with them, as sometimes happens to people who draw the intimacy of and confidences of others, precisely by not being intimate themselves. But I learned!

After that came the tightening of friendships, the increasing familiarity, the constant stimulation one experiences ib the company of vibrant, alive, and intelligent people. Then, in parties, weekends in beach houses, pleasant evenings, the friendships grew closer.

What I was experiencing was the living proof that youth existed and was beautiful, that youth involved energy, the pleasure of being in a group, the enjoyment of parties, frankness, and spontaneity. Before then, I had truly not ever known or felt any similar sensations.

Now I felt the wind in my hair, as I drove the open car into the ever-darkening night

The drive from Havana to Varadero Beach was a 3 hour affair, as one went through small fishing villages along the coast, where life moved slowly, with henequen plantations, with rows of spiny plants arranged in never-ending battle lines. Finally, after passing Matanzas, a sizable town with an udder-shaped bay, one enters the long, dandy peninsula jutting out into the sea, where Varadero is located. It was a sort of tropical Cape Cod with the same sparse beauty of its northern counterpart, but it was touched by the added advantage of its tropical appeal. Crystalline waves break upon miles of pure white sand. The town of Varadero itself, an original fishing village, had by then become a luxury resort area, with many beautiful summer homes, and some hotels catering to international tourists. It was to one of those houses where I had been invited. It belonged to Mimi, a cousin of Arsenio, whom I had met at the rehearsal. She was a well-dressed and beautifully mannered woman, well into her forties. Only later, I discovered that on meeting her, I had made the faux-pas of calling her "Senora", a title reserved for married women, instead of the appropriate "Senorita". She was not married.

As I drove up, the house was full of lights like an ocean liner floating in the darkness. It was just a few yards away from the crystalline water's edge, separated from it by a strip of very white sandy beach. Peals of laughter and sounds of conversation mingled with the soft roar of the mild surf. I entered and ny thoughts were buried in the sounds of greetings. I was lost again in a multitude of welcoming friends. In a little mezzanine, close to the door, Mimi was holding court with a small group, some of whose members I thought I recognized.

"Andres, you certainly look tired today" she said to one of them"
"Perhaps I am, you know the wear and tear of love" he replied.
"My dear, you sound like an aging machine".
"You would be surprised at what experience can do to a man"
"Well then, tell us about your experiences" said Mimi.
"Essentially, they deal with my basic malady"
"And may I ask what is that?

"I suffer from a chill of the soul".

"Poor man, is that contagious?"

"Only if I am made love to".

"Then I shall be careful not to", said Mimi. "Is it curable?'

"Yes, by totally ignoring it. Like a common cold".

"Can it get worse?"

"It might, if I feel I'm desired" replied Andres, briskly standing up.

'Andres, I think the trouble with you is that you have been eating too many frozen foods lately. Tomorrow we shall have a good roast, and I am sure you will immediately notice a change for the better in you".

There was good-natured laughter in the group as she gave as she gave me an affectionate hug and disappeared into the terrace. I moved on.

There must have been at least 15 persons in the house for the weekend. It came as no surprise to find out that it had only a few bedrooms, so everybody had to find a place to sleep as best they could, girls with girls, and boys with boys. I learned to expect anything from this new circle of friends. We were young, restless, and carefree and Mimi mi liked to have a crowd of widely different personalities always milling about her. The informality of the atmosphere, and the stimulation resulting from such an assortment, more than balanced the small discomfort. A philosophy of live-as-you-please dominated the house on such weekends.

Some went to bed at six in the morning, about the same time others were getting up to watch the sunrise. Lunch was served in several installments, from eleven in the morning, till five in the afternoon. Some late sleepers got up around noon, just about when others had their lunch and prepared for the afternoon siesta. It was a life with a devil-may-care attitude. We were intoxicated with the beauty of the beach, the wildness of our informal, young life, and with the fun of our own enmeshing personalities.

There are some people who, because of some peculiar trait in their character or mode of life, seem singularly displaced from the usual channels of human behavior. Not referring to the abnormal, the perverse, or the absurd, but rather to those driven by some unconscious impulse, to refuse to conform, to insist on asserting their own individual personalities and inclinations. It is from people like that we often learn and expand ourselves. It is they, who leave an ever-widening influence on us and make us grow. In this section of humanity, I have always felt a strong and absorbing interest, perhaps as a reaction to my own emotional childhood. Yet life often hides the coming of significant events, so that we experience them when least expected. How then was I to know how deeply our lives would become entangled in that group of people? How was I to plumb the movement of our respective paths, ultimately leading to a final resolution? The ripples of that warm spring night on the beach spread out to quietly affect my life in unexpected ways; in such subtle ways does fate move us like pieces on a chessboard.

The cool breezes blowing in from the sea were a welcome relaxation after the long drive on the prior day. Eventually I settled down in an armchair on the terrace, where Arsenio was discussing his plans for the coming stage production, which for him was nothing but a pretext to try something new: a plaything with which to amuse himself. Arsenio's quest in life was for personalities. The human being was the object of his hunt, not his prey, but the object of his interest; a never-ending search, as any who sets too high a standard. His was a hunt for the unicorn. His curiosity was directed at any new human possibility which could offer him a new experience, a new perspective, sometimes a new love. His saving grace was his charming spontaneity, his boyish ingenuity, genuine and not faked. His ebullient personality lent its tone to the whole company, and his imagination and wild fancy kept the group on its feet. A few disagreed with his views, some envied him, but everyone liked him. He was also one of those lucky people in whom a vibrant native imagination was combined with enormous inherited wealth from sugar plantations. It was this that provided feasible ways in which the wild fancies of his imagination could be transformed into practical reality. The result was an impressive spectacle to behold.

I was musing upon these thoughts, when I realized I was getting drowsy and when Arsenio left, I drifted into a nice siesta.

Next morning was beautiful, a warm sun shone on the dazzling beach in front of the house. Noises from below indicated that someone had to be up and about. Washing up and putting on a pair of shorts, I came downstairs where there was a group of 7 or 8 other people congregated in the open terrace facing the sea.

Maria was sitting on the terrace railing, adopting one of her fashion model poses. She acted as if she had seen, as a girl, a Vogue magazine model in one of those impossible stilted poses, which might be called something like "going to the tropics" or some such reeking dribble, and had thereafter never been able to outgrow it. She had a diseased longing for fashionable clothes and changed her whole attire at least three times daily, yet never seemed to pick the ones that really suited her.

Marita and Magdalena were engaged in a lively discussion on the relative merits of their respective nail polishes. Henry was sunning his tan, lithe body in a lounge chair. "I suspect both of my dogs, Ruby and Mota of being both Lesbians", Arsenio commented as I walked in with a breakfast tray and sat down in an empty chair. The remark brought renewed chuckles from everyone and an icy stare from Mimi.

"What do you mean? Can you prove it?"

"I suppose I can't, but didn't you hear all of the rattling and scratching last night? Shortly afterwards, Mota came into my room with an enormous stare and distended pupils. What else do you suppose that means? Sex, sex everywhere, even the dogs!"

"As usual, Arsenio. You are distorting reality to suit your own unbridled mind".

"But I assure you, it is true!"

"Nonsense".

As punctuation to her remark, a loud yelp issued from under the terrace and both dogs came rushing out, one chasing the other with demonstrable interest. A chorus of laughter. At this, Concha readily became nervous as she clutched her ancient female Pekingese, which by this time was positively excited by all the noise and barking. Concha was the widow of an ambassador long dead, a woman of about 65 years of age, but still very active. The polished marks of long years of life within the diplomatic corps could be detected in her, mixed now with a humorous, earthy streak which made her a wonderful companion in any group. She thoroughly enjoyed weekends on the beach, even if her company was half her age at most. Her life was partially devoted to her hideous female Pekingese dog, which she had acquired many years before. By this time, it had had all of the real and imagined canine diseases a dog could possibly have. The most obvious one was a constant, nervous twitch in her face, and a declared aggressiveness not only to everyone, but also to everything in sight, since at its great age, it could hardly distinguish between the two. Only her owner was exempt from these attacks. Any loud noise, or moving object would get her excited beyond measure, producing an uncontrolled series of growls and twitchings which made it look wildly ridiculous.

The warmth of the terrace had been enough to warrant cocktails, so now the houseboy came in with a tray of cooling daiquiris. This prompted Arsenio to go on his monologue.

"I am definitely growing older, Mimi, I am sure of it" Arsenio kept on saying. "I feel my hair receding and my teeth getting looser. All this I get in spite of leading a quiet, chaste life. It makes one wonder whether I'm losing the best years of my life. Maybe if I practiced all sorts of debauchery, I would look younger. The rottenness of this world!

What do you think?"

Marta, in her modish pose, kept on watching the idle bathers and strollers in the uncrowded beach in front of us. Someone came up with the idea that champagne would taste better if you simultaneously spilled a bit of it over your body while you were drinking it. The taste would then be absorbed not only by your mouth, but also through every single pore of your body. This pilgrim idea was enough to get Marta to abandon her "going to the tropics" pose and going to the kitchen, she fetched several bottles of Piper Heidseck, and aided by

Maria, she poured some of the effervescent liquid over us while we sat there, motionless, with open mouths, our bare skin and chest shining with globules of the draining wine. The pop of corks, the general alarum, and the women's shrieks were enough to provoke a violent attack of the shakes in Concha's lap dragoness, so she hastened to steal away from the scene while holding the monster aloft. The noise awakened the rest of the guests, and shortly afterwards, the terrace was crowded with the still slumbering newcomers, who at noon, were trying to decide half consciously whether to have breakfast first, or down their pre-lunch daiquiris directly, and forget about breakfast. A new day was in full swing.

It developed amidst the usual abandon and informality, through the sultry hours of a tropical afternoon; then a long siesta, another swim in the early evening, then dressing up for cocktails and dinner at one of the local beach hotels, dancing into the evening, and some tours along the local night spots usually full, of tourists, European displaced nobility, local gigolos trying to make a night of it, wealthy husbands from Havana having a Saturday evening fling away from home, and deserted mistresses looking for new attachments.

But more than just this constantly changing panorama of human faces, I loved those weekends at the beach for the unspoiled glimpse of sparse beauty and deserted beaches. The barren, sandy peninsula had a charm of its own. I had sometime read that the ancient Greeks thought that at the stroke of twelve, at noon, when the sun is its highest point in the sky, the spirits of the dead would come forth upon the world and for a few brief moments partake of the world of the living. Strange belief to modern mind, where a more fitting moment for such an occurrence would appear to be at the stroke of midnight, when the darkness and the mystery of the night shadows would seem to better provide the dreaded qualities associated with the ghostly and the supernatural.

Yet once you have been in the tropics, you realize that the Greeks knew what they were talking about, even if Greece is not situated exactly in the tropics. In the tropics, morning in the countryside is usually born in the midst of wet, fresh vapors, accompanied by the cries of wild birds and animals, and the general noise of life around you gradually increases, as the sun rises in the sky. Finally at noon, as the hot sun shines directly overhead, a peculiar stillness invades the land. You no longer hear the sounds of animals or birds, and stillness pervades the earth for some time. You stand in the sizzling heat with no shadows, since the sun is directly overhead, and looking in front of you, one sees the landscape vibrating in a haze as the waves of heat rising from the ground, distort all normal proportions. Not a breeze stirs then, and you feel as if the vapors from some strong exotic liquor had gone to your head. Not a sound is heard, except perhaps the low, ominous hum of some flying insect, whizzing about you, displaying a bulky, multi-colored body.

There are few spectacles in nature more beautiful than a shallow pool of transparent crystalline sea water above a sandy bottom, upon which the full moon displays arabesques in glassy, movable shapes. It is the ideal situation for the appearance of the supernatural. The Greeks also apparently realized this as well. On the other hand, midnight in the tropics is full of noise and life, earthly life, the hooting of birds and insects, the rumble of animals on the prowl, and the clear full moon in a starry sky, hardly seem proper for a ghostly appearance. The time-honored tropical siesta is perhaps a psychological as well as physical recognition of the supernatural qualities of the tropical noon.

Other weekends at the beach followed, always in a mood of fevered eagerness, as well as in other occasions where I met Mimi and her friends. Labor union disputes at the factory kept me occupied and forced several temporary defections from that group of friends.

Shortly thereafter, I had gone several times to super with Magdalena, whose company I had always enjoyed. She had an inner exuberance, which when properly stimulated, and without the slightest provocation, enveloped her and was transmitted to all those around her. Even though she was not exactly beautiful, in a classical sense, the pristine quality of her free-flowing joy fitted her pleasant face. People in any group sought her out to enjoy her extroversion, perhaps to forget their own self-consciousness in the liveliness of her manner. Her passions were many and strong, her beliefs simple but sincere, her sorrows few, and were hidden behind the walls of her uncontained vivacity. Greeting you after only a few days' interval, she would act as if she had not seen you for years and was relishing the encounter; her vivacity was held within such limits as would not make then appear preposterous or faked; her sincerity so obvious as to preclude all suspicions of falsity.

At bottom, she was a non-conformist, setting high store on simple pleasures, enjoying nature, flowers and trees in a way that only a sensitive woman can. These very special qualities, however, sometimes set her apart from the circles of stereotyped sophistication in which she moved. Others tried to draw her into their common patterns, sometimes reading their own defects into her qualities. What drew me into the circle of her light? Perhaps the remains of a sense of humor which found in her a kindred echo. While I had known her for some time, and frequently gone out with her in mixed company, it was quite suddenly that sitting in my car one day by a lovely summer sunset, we found ourselves—quite simply—to be lovers.

Our relationship was characterized by swift changes as a result of her volatile personality. There was never a dull moment. Sometimes she delighted in coaxing herself to displays of inexhaustible melodrama; she would mope around for days, exuding an air of gloom, and while she seemed sincere in her actual or imagined sorrows, she could not help but entertain a slight suspicion that at bottom, she was enjoying it for the attention she received. Watching her during one of these periods, I imagined some passe' prima donna of the stage or screen, someone like Bernhardt or Duse, reclining in a theatrical divan, hair disheveled and crying out: "How wretched I am!" The scene was tinted with unspeakable hilarity. At such times, I teased her into hot rages by refusing to be impressed, and by ridiculing her little scene with some a propos comment; Noel Coward's famous line: "Women should be hit regularly, like a gong" was one of the ones I used that usually produced violent results, although of course I never hit her! In mock seriousness, I pointed out that most of her sorrows could be dispelled by a well-directed kick to her mental buttocks, and she could not easily bear the tension of being suddenly deprived of her tragic airs. In the end, she laughed with me and returned to her normal ebullient self. At least she had a fabulous virtue: she could never bore anyone! It is the perfect quality in a woman. It was that character, that character which persuaded me to marry her...and then to divorce her.... later in my life. Events that happened later on, years after I had divorced her proved that my decision to separate from her was without doubt, the correct one. After that, it was very clear to me that the way of a conventional marriage was certainly not my way.

Back in Havana, I renewed my visits to Arsenio's house on different occasions. Sometime while sitting on the terrace, having a drink, Bonzo the lion would interrupt the quiet with one of his lazy, yawning, but quite loud roars from his pen in the back yard. It sounded so completely out of place an African lion's roar in this warm, civilized tropical suburb. It was as if something tore your universe apart. You look at your drink and wondered: was that a real lion? You felt as if while bathing in a private swimming pool, you found yourself facing a fully grown shark!. Arsenio had bought Bonzo a year before from a Central American farm which specialized in growing and selling real lions, panthers and other wild animals to zoos and private collectors.

Coming originally as a cub, Bonzo had become an imposing beast that had to be quartered in a special enclosure in the back of the garden. It was fairly tame and would not wantonly attack anybody or anything, yet it still retained the native freedom of his breed and you approached him always with care. Still, he was an imposing sight to anyone not aware of his presence, especially if they suddenly met it face to-face in a living room.

It became one of Arsenio's favorite tricks to invite several young men and women to dinner at his home for an evening of company, drinks and fine dining. Of course there had to be *de rigueur* at least one chaperone as well, because no proper young woman at that time would want to be seen going out with men without a chaperone being present; otherwise her reputation would be ruined.

The climax of those evenings came sometime during dinner, the whole company sitting down in a long dinner table, in an elegant dining room in his house, when the kitchen door would suddenly open and Bonzo the lion, would stroll in, sometimes with an earth-shaking roar. The reaction at that event from the unsuspecting guests would range anywhere from utter stupefaction, to frantic escape maneuvers. It usually took a while for Arsenio to calm the guests, and assure them that the lion was harmless, and indeed the beast was tame and never bit or harmed anyone.

A similar situation, with even more import, sometimes happened at the summer house in Varadero Beach (which I have described above). He would walk along the beach, with the lion on a leash, to the complete amazement of anyone who was there. Or even worse, he would put the lion in the back seat of his open Thunderbird convertible, and drive to one of the big international hotels on the beach, and proceed to walk through the entrance, lobby, and cocktail terrace, which were usually full of international tourists. He had suitably tipped the hotel employees and managers to let him proceed undisturbed. Again, the whole thing did not imply danger to anyone, and no negative incident ever happened. It was, in a way, a reflection of the easy live-and-let-live life among those tropics at that time. But one could never forget the total incongruity, wildness, and just sheer enjoyment of being present while incidents like this were happening; they are truly unforgettable memories.

And so, the afternoons went by on those days by the beach. People who have never been to the West Indies imagine scenes of intense heat, with the perfect calm of a picture postcard, where oceans on summer days lap at the white sands with small, slow ripples. It is usually an image of stillness in the heat of the afternoon, when motion is impossible and unthinkable. While actually this is generally true, it would be hard for them to imagine another scene, equally true, when an autumn northeasterly wind, a "norte", (a north) as the natives call it, comes crashing in and in a gray metallic leap raises high waves against the coast. The wind whistles through the deserted beach where only the shrill cries of the sandpipers are heard. This bleak picture may last several days and is quite common in the winter months. When a "norte" comes in, the whole character of the place changes: in Havana, people put on their winter coats, and tend to walk in quick fast steps: life takes on a faster tempo, you think of new important things. It is as if suddenly you were reminded of the vastness of the world from that warm isolated heaven you had inhabited, like a sudden knock on the door, or a swift change of pace.

A DESCRIPTION OF SOME FAMILIAR PERSONALITIES NOTED AT COLLEGE

1. The Hypocrite or the False One.

He goes along proclaiming his eminent qualities, his wisdom and his dignity. He wastes no opportunity to show how much he knows. He has the airs of a great man, who disdains his inferiors because they are less intelligent. He even deludes those who meet him for the first time and don't know him well. It pleases him to ask an infinite number of silly questions, without any sense or purpose, but he believes that evidently demonstrates his interest and knowledge. Each time he has to answer a question, he does so with a grandiloquent style and his stumbling accent. He skips shaving for a few days, believing that makes evident his discolored virility. His desire is to earn money when he graduates from college. His characteristic greeting is "Do you know what I did the other day?" or "Do you who I was introduced to?

2. The Disillusioned One.

He had a joke to tell each minute and he was always laughing. He was elected President or Secretary of numberless freshman associations and clubs. His name was easy to pronounce and frequent in the popular conversation of the class. Even the professors laughed with him. Everybody was his friend, until the day exams came. He did not pass a single one. He took to walking about with the neck of his coat raised up to his ears, with a glum expression on his face. He talks to no one and is a disillusioned one.

3. The Religious One.

He sits every afternoon with a Bible older than he in the library and takes notes for an imaginary conference about the Old Testament. His expression is that of the statues of saints, disfigured by the divinity and good will that men attributed to such figures. His conversation involves the fourth article of Genesis, or psalm 24. He wonders what happened to a fellow student who did not attend the last meeting of some religious congregation. He condemns any insignificant comment or action made by anybody that might appear impious, and considers it as an attempt to violate proper morals.

IV

FULLNESS
(1972-2007)-(Age 40-75)

THE COMING OF REVOLUTION

I was working in Havana, as I will explain below, during the last phase of General Fulgencio Batista, who had taken over the government of Cuba in a military coup, replacing the normally elected President at that time. The military government was characterized by theft of public moneys, army and police control of the country, and mismanagement of public affairs, so much so that it created a substantial opposition from many segments of the population. This was evidenced by an attack on the presidential palace in Havana, residence of Batista, when a group of radical, armed revolutionaries entered the palace, shooting and killing a number of guards, and proceeded up the central ascending staircase to the upper floor living quarters, where the president resided. They were unsuccessful as they were shot down and killed by additional guards who prevented their ascent. This describes the atmosphere reigning at that time in Cuba, added to the oppressive humidity of what should be a peaceful isle.

Eventually, Fidel Castro started an opposition organization which landed an expeditionary force in an isolated area of the island and eventually took over. Batista fled to Miami.

A New Year's Eve Party

Jon, an American friend who I met when he was working in Cuba, representing an American company, invited me to a New Year's Eve party at his home in Havana, on December 31, 1959. where a number of his American and Cuban friends were present. Some of them I had met before, and we were enjoying the celebration when someone knocked at the door, and shouted: 'Batista is gone! Fidel Castro has taking over!' A new era had I fact begun!

The company I was working for in the USA decided, and I had accepted, to be transferred as a member of the manufacturing supervision in a factory they owned and operated in Havana and I functioned as such for several years. Eventually, after transferring to another factory, I ended up as manufacturing manager in the start-up of a large operation producing ceramic pieces in a large scale, like ceramic toilets for homes, ceramic sinks, bathtubs, and similar ceramic objects. The ceramic pieces, after being formed and shaped out of clay, additives, and glazes, had to then be "baked" in a large, one block plus long oven, where the pieces were loaded in a railed train system, and pulled along, as were baked and finished by a series of flaming jets along the path. The jets brought the pieces to a high temperature as they moved along the path and produced finished glazed items. Of course it took qualified employees to operate such complex machines, and at minimum they had to know not only how to read and write, but have the essential ability to read and understand temperatures and pressures, and react as necessary to the varying conditions of the elaborate manufacturing process. For this reason, I did not trust the Personnel Department of the plant to do a satisfactory job, so I insisted with the General Manager that I had to do the personal interviews of every person hired, for both supervisory management and factory employees as well.

I wanted to make sure that we would start with qualified people aboard in a highly technical environment. It would be dangerous in that environment to start up with unqualified personnel.

So I did interview and check references personally on every new hire. As a result, we started the process without any problem or negative incident, and the plant was working satisfactorily and efficiently.

The general manager was himself a product of the revolution, where he had had some part to play in the revolt against the government of Batista and had been rewarded for his participation with the presumably well-paid job, but without him having a technical or engineering or even plain management background at all. So after a while, he came one day into my office and asked that from then on, all employees had to be interviewed and hired by the Personnel Manager alone without my approval. The person in charge of Personnel was another one like him, given a job for his participation in the revolution, but with any manufacturing qualifications or experience either. I knew that that was a prescription for trouble, serious trouble that I could not accept. In fact they wanted to hire an older man as an oven operator, who could not read or write! He would have been unable to intelligently operate and run that piece of complex machinery without being even able to read a temperature! So I had no choice but to resign my job as Manufacturing Manager and that was the end of my connection with that operation.

But, no surprise! Sometime later I heard the news that the oven in that factory had overheated, the flames kept going on much beyond operating temperatures, and the oven roof had collapsed, immobilizing the whole operation in a major disaster. I never found what eventually happened, because I left the country by then.

What is Important Now?-(Age 57)

This is a time in my life (in Nov 1989) which the primordial, classic worries that affect most men and have affected me as well, have now been essentially resolved, to wit:

- The basic worries about financial security and economic sustenance are essentially resolved. Calamity could strike at any time but security is here in that I don't have to worry about where my nest meal is coming from, and the future is essentially secure.

- Physical health, as well as self-esteem, are on the way up.
- Ontological concern about relationships, politics, religion, friends, behavior, positions, and the rest—which so concern us all, are mostly resolved. I am someone who knows who he is, what he wants, and what is of value to him.
- The need to cater or to depend on others for personal or economic sustenance is no longer there. Personal freedom for me is relatively large It is also more so and more important as time goes on.
- So what is important now?
  - Ecstasy. Learning and experiencing it.
  - Union with the other. Dissolution of the split, the gap.
  - Reduction of anger levels.
  - Close friendships.
  - Growth of the spirit.
  - Experiencing selfless, ego-less love.

Cesar Calvo, from "INO MOXO".-"Then you will see that the masks are always under the face".

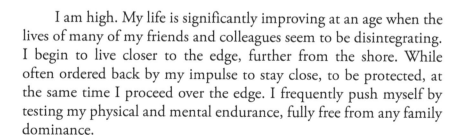

I am high. My life is significantly improving at an age when the lives of many of my friends and colleagues seem to be disintegrating. I begin to live closer to the edge, further from the shore. While often ordered back by my impulse to stay close, to be protected, at the same time I proceed over the edge. I frequently push myself by testing my physical and mental endurance, fully free from any family dominance.

There seems to be a law of the mind that you become what you resist. If you resist your mother, for example, you become identified with her and her attitudes. When you submit to, resist, hate, or identify with something—you become attached to it. So it seems to be that you must go past the point of resistance (and attachment to) these issues, and decide to leave them behind and go past them into new, freer, and more enjoyable territory.

——————————⊙—————————

William B. Yeats.- *"The best lack all conviction, while the worst are full of passionate intensity".*

TERENCE MCKENNA

I had the good fortune to meet Terence at a seminar he held near my home. I was very impressed by his intelligence, sense of humor, wisdom and delivery, and with time developed into a personal friendship with him that was very productive and rewarding to me and continued until his untimely death from cancer, if I remember right. During that time, along with two other partners, we organized a series of seminars held here in the USA as well as in some foreign countries, which were extremely successful and attracted hundreds of participants. I was the organizer, while my partners were the speakers at those events, and they were extremely qualified and excellent presenters. It was a very productive and interesting period in my life, and I benefitted from the gain of several wonderful friends. Here are some of my favorite quotes from Terence that I jotted down in his talks:

> **1988.-** * "There are a myriad ways to get distracted from the pith, the essence of your being: by addicting, consuming, obsessing, controlling".

- "Ritual is what you do, when you don't know what else to do".
- The universe is such an enormously complex thing, of such an unfathomable meaning, that we cannot hope to understand it. The tremendum surrounds us at every turn, but it is hidden by the fabric of everyday life"

1989.- "People are not machines, but given the opportunity to act as such, they will do so. We tend to addict to the familiar, so unless we deliberately disturb and perturb our life, we tend to automate, and consciousness contracts and shrinks".

1990.- "Existential worry is preposterous. We don't know enough about it to worry".

Through Terence, I met two other outstanding men: Jonathan Ott and Robert Montgomery. We soon discovered that we all had mutual interests, and so the four of us decided to organize and hold a series of conferences and seminars open to the public on the subject of Ethnobotany and Chemistry that were run from 1994 to 2001. This was a subject that Rob had had some experience already because he had run some of these meetings under the name "Botanical Preservation Corps" which we initially continued to use, after a while changing it to "Entheobotany", and also to "Alchemical Arts". They were held in different locations around the world. Including the USA, Canada, Central and South America and Hawaii, and consisted of series of presentations and discussions led by world-renowned scientists and research people, and lasted for a week each. The locations were in suitable hotels with restaurants, usually in proximity to forests and plants, often in tropical environments. We were successful in attracting top-level presenters in our programs, including people like Albert Hoffman, Alexander Shulgin, Richard Evans Schultes, Peter Furst, Kary Mullis, Bruce Damer, Paul Stamets, Christian Ratsch and many others, all widely known in their respective fields, as respected scientists, some were Nobel Laureates, and many were top professors in first class universities throughout the world.

I acted mainly as a manager/organizer of these projects, while the other three of us acted as actual presenters in the program, because they were all experts in their respective areas of it. My job was to issue announcements, receive and record registrations, deal with the operators of the locations where the seminars were held, and provide overall management to the project.

It was an unparalleled opportunity for me to meet some very special human beings in close quarters, many luminaries in their own fields, some quite famous, and see some places of the world which I would have never seen otherwise. We held the conferences often near locations with ancient ruins or historical places of significance, having hotels with suitable accommodations and meeting rooms nearby. It was a memorable experience for me and one that I would not have missed, and relish without qualification. After 10 years of these, Terence unfortunately died from cancer, and we decided we had to move on in our livers, so the conferences were discontinued.

Some Thoughts

1. Fatigue is not a natural consequence of living. If one feels fatigue often, something is off or not right. One needs to find out what that is.

2. Whining is like hitching another car to long team of complaints, hurts, and wounds. That doesn't heal anything. For healing to take place, some other change needs to happen.

3. Intimacy with oneself, cannot solve anybody else's problems with their lovers, family, etc. All one can do is offer support but not solve their intimacy problems

M.MEADE/ J. HILLMAN- "THE ACORN"

My notes from a talk by them that I attended:

> *"The established dogma is that what we are is because of our parents.*
>
> *Another way to think about this, is that at birth we are already an acorn that has all its future destiny written within it already, and that the oddities that we experience as we grow up; shyness, unconformity, isolation, are all strategies we assume to protect the acorn. Actually ancestors are often more important than parents. The more "initiated" one is, the less important the parents become—they are then seen as just human beings, suffering just like us.*
>
> *When faced with an unsurmountable choice, an either/or, come back with an unrelated answer. To answer the question "marry me now or not", answer with: "I'm hungry and need some food now". That shifts the paradigm and gives you time to consider your action."*

LADY CHATTERLEY, on reaching such a state of emotional abandonment and bereavement, finally realizes that she was "to be had for the taking".

ON BOOK PUBLISHING

I have always been an avid reader of books, on all subjects, from all authors. There were two books that I read in middle age that struck me as especially interesting, well written and memorable One was written in Spanish by the Peruvian author Cesar Calvo and it dealt with events taking place in the wilderness of the Peruvian

Amazon. The book narrated the story of Ino Moxo, a particularly gifted Amazon shaman and healer who met Cesar and told his story to him. Cesar's eloquent and poetic prose was far beyond anything I had ever read and it contained a deep sense of the human and of the transcendental. I thought I might translate into English and thus I wrote to him in Iquitos, in care of his publisher from nine years earlier. I heard nothing back from him for over a year. The thought of a possible translation receded. Then I received an unexpected letter from Cesar. He was in Lima and had just received my year-old letter. Things, including letters, move slower in the Amazon! We connected; I went to Peru to meet Cesar in person. The man in person far exceeded my expectations in vitality, heart, and imagination. He had a wide circle of friends in all classes of society, and he was grandiose, to say the least, in his relationships with them. In fact he organized a banquet in one of the local restaurants, inviting some of them, to offer me a welcome to Peru as his special guest, and he dedicated all of his time to me while I was there. From that meeting in Lima came the publication of his book: "The Three Halves of Ino Moxo", now available in my English translation of the work, published by Inner Traditions International, in Rochester, Vermont. It deals with the life and times of Ino Moxo, a native healer and sorcerer whom Cesar presumable met in person and wrote his book about. Ino Moxo is described as an extremely intelligent and powerful practitioner of ancient Amazonian folklore, which is quite challenging and interesting to read and think about. The descriptions are 1beyond imagination and his adventures have a limitless range.

My second experience in book translation and publishing came about when I came across and read the fascinating book "A Brief History of Drugs" written in Spanish by Prof. Antonio Escohotado, which covered humanity's checkered and often ambivalent relationship with drugs, from the role of the opium poppy in ancient Mesopotamia, through the mystery cult of Eleusis in Greece, the wars in China, the persecution of medieval herbalist witches, up to the present. I contacted the author and we agreed on my translating the book into English, which was the published by and available from the Park Street Press, in Rochester, Vermont.

After those two, I then felt I had accumulated enough material to write my own book "Hypomnemata: stories, fables, memories", which was published in 2014 by Xlibris (www.Xlibris.com). That was really just what the title implied: a collection of fictional stories, dreams, visions, word plays, metaphors, and personal memories about the human predicament. This partly explains the background for the book you have in hand now.

At this time, I am about to publish another book "The Invisible Theater", which describes what happened when a group of adventurous men put together a theatrical presentation. It is described elsewhere in this book.

"Think your thoughts,
Feel your feelings
Do your actions."
> Don't feel your thoughts, or think your feelings,
> or do either with your actions.

ROBERT BLY.- (1988)-(AGE 56)

I had the privilege and good luck to have attended several of Robert Bly's seminars given around this time. They were directed generally to men, and addressed mens' problems, although by no means putting down the feminine. Bly was a gregarious, outspoken man, and I enjoyed his presentations they brought a lot of light to my perception of things at that time. I am very grateful for his teachings. Here are some of my notes I excerpted from his talks:

> "Do not blame yourself for **not** doing anything when you were very young (a child);

You **survived**!. That is the only thing you could do!".

"in childhood, the issue is not elegance, but survival".

"It is better to explore unknown territory alone, without a guide, rather than to use a map made by others".

"After 35, we develop starfish ability to regenerate missing parts of our psychic bodies. We can regenerate missing parts that have been severed".

A PLAN OF ACTION FOR THE NEXT 5 YEARS.- (1992)-(AGE 60)

Here are some notes written by me and addressed to myself:

1. Love Yourself.- Accept yourself for what you are. Don't let your ambition make you feel bad because of what you are not. What you are is quite good!.

2. You are a builder, an engineer by nature. You are not only that, but you are that. Rejoice in it. Express yourself in it. Build. Repair. Expand. Express your creativity in it, build rooms, construct sun-dials, install new things.

3. Stop Worrying.- Stop the anxiety, stop the needless stress on your system. By stopping concern about money, maintenance, etc. You will be all right. This concern is affecting your system by showing up as high blood pressure and high cholesterol.

4. Take Action.- To achieve in reality what needs to be done. Don't worry. Act. Do what needs to be done rather than think about it.

5. Plan your days in small sections and set yourself one small goal or task at a time, and then complete it. Don't let worry about "the big picture" confuse and just set one objective

at a time. And then <u>do it</u> Satisfaction will come from completing one job at a time, well and thoroughly.

6. <u>Allow time for creative tasks</u>.- In you, creativity doesn't need to be painting or writing. It can also be planting, repairing, building things. making beautiful living spaces. starting a new small business, mending something broken, creating a more comfortable room, building a sun-dial. Rejoice in the beauty that you create and that others admire.

7. <u>Let love control you less</u>. Let go. It will come when it comes- be less frantic about it and it will come easier. It is NOT as important as you have thought it is in your life. Love yourself more, and others will follow in loving you more.

8. <u>Take care of your body</u>.- Eat well and with balanced food. Jog steadily at least 3 times per week. Don't over-drink. Eat good meals.

9. <u>Make your life a work of art</u>.- Make it colorful, balanced, exciting, stimulating, rewarding, a pleasure to contemplate. It is the biggest gift you can give anyone: to set a space so challenging that they can share a part of it with you, and use whatever they can of it.

10. <u>Do frequent meditations</u>.- They will center and ground you.

11. <u>Stop the chatter of your mind</u>.- One way in which you can do that is by reading instead.

<u>**Source Unknown**</u>.- *"Never allow anyone to <u>shame you. Never, for any reason, under any circumstance</u>".

- "Doctors are not very far from being just glorified plumbers".
- "*Los hombres acaban por hacer lo que quieren, o creer que asi lo hacen*"---(Men end up by doing what they want, or believing that are doing so").

PROGENY?

My usual custom when younger was to go to gymnasiums several times a week for physical exercise: weight lifting and jogging, for which I am very grateful because the practice kept in proper body weight, a sane body, above all with relative freedom from common diseases as I got older. Part of the routine at gyms was to take stem bath and shower after exercise. I very much enjoyed the steam baths. Perhaps because of that, I became interested in the Native American use of sweat lodges: small constructions holding several seated persons, with a central fire in the middle which was the doused gently with water, causing a large volume of steam in the enclosure. Originally sweat lodges were led by a native shaman or priest, who recited incantations and led brief ceremonies during the time people were in the lodge, which could easily last 2-3 hours; In other words, equivalent to a steam bath. I enjoyed participating in some of these sweat lodges, and eventually came to build one in a suitable property and run them myself with a group of interested people, although I never pretended to be a native shaman. While leading one of these one time, I met a young man, Manfred, who was a participant, and he was so much impressed by the whole sweat lodge procedure, that he remained for a while after it was over, asking me questions about it. We hit it off very well and as a consequence arranged to meet afterwards to continue our conversation. I found him to be inquisitive, young, agile in body and mind, and concerned about the general questions about life that a young man like him faces. He wanted answers, and was not getting him from his father, because his family were ardent Mormons, with very strong belief systems, that did not suit their son.

As time passed, the friendship grew and strengthened, and gradually I found myself in a place of orienting, guiding and supporting his development, almost as his father would. Here I was, not ever wanting a child, and yet in effect almost playing the role of an actual father. To my surprise, I enjoyed it, and I consider a blessing that the friendship and connection continued for the rest of my life and to this day, always productive, interesting and often challenging but always in a positive sense. I think of him as a blessing in my life.

Ruben Dario. - *"How painful it is to love, and not know how to express it"*.

CARLO COCCIOLI.- ABOUT "FABRIZIO LUPO"

About this time in my life, I came across a book written by an Italian author, Carlo Coccioli, published in a Spanish translation in 1953--------- a novel about a person describing a loving relationship about a character named Fabrizio Lupo. The tone of the written word is lush, vibrant with romantic feeling, full of concern about another human being, and willing to have no limits in fulfilling his love, which unfortunately leads him to his death. The language is so rich that it struck a familiar chord in the feelings I was experiencing myself at that time. I was 'blown overboard' by the richness of expression and depth of feeling. It made a big impression on me. Here are a few quotes from it:

"I want to love you, I want to live with you, I want to give myself wholly to you, but I want to be the one that gives. I want to be in the cage of your affection, and you must admit it, Fabrizio, that it means unarguably a cage; nevertheless, it is I who must love, who must accept being caged".

"Why have I been made this way? Whose fault is it? This has lasted for a long time and no one suspected that such a violent pain pressed upon me; because I suffered not as a human being can suffer (a human being who always retains the possibility of revealing his torment, but more like a toad, hurt and solitary, or a sick dog, or an ant".

"I have always believed in the impenetrability of sentiments. We think that we can understand what another human being is experiencing, while the truth is we only capture the part that is familiar to us. I do not seek your understanding, what I seek is your help".

"It is important that a book be born in pain" *(An interesting thought, but one with which I don't necessarily agree—my note—KAS)*

MichaelAngelo.- *"Dove vai— sempre son teco, ti troverei quand'io fossi ben cieco".*
"Where you go—I will always be with you, I shall find you, even if I was truly blind".

Manuel de Falla—(from "El Amor Brujo")

*"Lo mismo que el fuego fatuo
Lo mismito es el querer
Le huyes y te persigue
Le llamas y echa a correr"*

———————————◉———————————

"The same as the will-o'-the-wisp
the same thing is love,
you flee from it, and it follows,
you call for it, and it runs away".

Benjamin Disraeli

"The greatest good you can do for another is not just to share your riches, but to reveal to him his own'

Anais Nin

"Each friend represents a world in us, a world possibly not born until they arrive, and it is only by this meeting that a new world is born".

Budenweiss

"The man who is worthy of being a leader of men, will never complain of the stupidity of his helpers, or of the ingratitude of mankind, or of the unappreciation of the people. These things are all a part of the great game of life, and to meet them and not go down before them in discouragement and defeat is the final proof of power."

Seven Lessons learned during the past year (January 1999.-(Age 67)

1. A certain fearlessness is the only proper attitude, in the face of one's inadequacies.
2. Live in a state of imaginative opulence.
3. Don't run around with anyone who doesn't love you.
4. Being brave is one thing that one never regrets.
5. The mechanics of death are trivial; the meaning of death could be profound.
6. Never take love, without giving it in return.
7. Never give love, without receiving it in return.

WALT WHITMAN

> "I see in you the estuary that enlarges and spreads itself grandly as it pours into the great sea".

I could not have written any words more promising and encouraging that those quoted above by Walt Whitman, which I used to give myself permission to explore life and my capabilities without limit for many years,

DECEMBER 2000.- (AGE 68). AUTOMATIC WRITING

In a group of men, we practiced <u>automatic writing</u>, that is, writing down a paragraph of whatever words or phrases came into your mind automatically, without any selection or censorship, leaving out any cogent or conscious thoughts, impressions or pictures that may come in one's mind from the day's activity. The point is to filter out anything rational and let out purely unconscious material. It can be an interesting and challenging exercise because it lets you know what unconscious material is running loose through your mind at that particular time. This is the paragraph I wrote:

> *"Stay frozen in death, mea culpa. Nonsense, will not follow rules but mules will neither follow asses or horses, but sometimes carts, but that might not make wheels rotate. My! Oh my! what this will do to turkeys!."*

WILLIAM REICH

He saw evidence everywhere of somatized trauma. He felt that many people were suffering from it, but that most everyone had tacitly agreed not to notice that fact, and as a consequence no one was having a real experience, as long as they were not, themselves, exposed to their own anomalies. He made a list of symptoms, in people, of the anomalies he was referring to. The following two struck me as particularly motable:

- *Loud, obtrusive laughter.
- *Unvarying, dull friendliness

Cuban Popular Saying.- How black is black?
"Black as the night in which the pig was lost".

JAMES HILLMAN AND MICHAEL MEADE

Notes I wrote down from a seminar led by them that I attended:

"There can be no education, unless there is a psychological education. There can be no psychological education unless it addresses the relationship between the limited ego and the much bigger self. Fulfillment comes when you realize that there is something golden in you: the royal in you".

A PSYCHEDELIC TRIP

In my earlier years, I was too busy with my work and my career to try any experience with psychedelics, nor was I particularly interested in having any such experience. It was into my fortieth year, when I read some writings about the subject and I thought I might as well try it sometime. Through a mutual acquaintance, I contacted a woman who at that time was acting as a caretaker and general housekeeper of a large estate, the property of a a Los Angeles family who used it only some weekends during the year. So, I made arrangements with her to lead me and sit with me during a session where I ingested some psychoactive mushrooms. She was very kind and helpful, and she set me up in a comfortable bed, next to a large picture window, overlooking a marvelous setting in the Big Sur area of the California coast, among a grove of Sequoia trees, with the background below being a sharp cliff overlooking the Pacific Ocean. The setting was nothing less than ideal.

I put the dried mushroom stems and caps in my mouth, and began chewing and swallowing them; I noticed a slightly bitter taste, like seaweed, slightly acid and bitter. Noting happened for about one-half hour. Then, perception began to change. The colors in the room began to intensify. A wall of stones on one side of the room began to change in appearance and show different patterns of color. I began to see blobs of color in my peripheral vision. A wooden wall in the back of the room began to show a grid—the wall deepened and showed a hole opening up into a space resembling a gothic cathedral. As I looked into the upper wall, little heads began to appear crawling out of the wall, and then bodies of small dwarves, entities, animal-like beings that began to creep down the wall and play around the room. I marveled at what I was seeing! Suddenly the pet cat of my woman friend came into the room, but the cat had three distinct and separate heads! I couldn't believe what I was seeing!

Very intense images appeared in that space, heads and bodies with exaggerated borders and intense gaudy colors. The sense of depth and perspective was affected and I began to have difficulty in determining verticality, balance and proportion. By this time there was a strong sense of imbalance, and I felt somewhat silly, giggly, and not in control of anything, but in a good way. There was a slight feeling of nausea in my belly, but not particularly disagreeable. I felt as if I was transported to the hot Big Sur baths, and sitting in the warm water up to my neck, I was very mellow, things appeared to be fluid, I felt slightly drunk. A canopy of colored lights appeared over my head as in a mosaic: reds, greens. blues, yellows. As I looked up at the sky, constellations appeared to take on new forms and outlines.

A big butterfly shape, formed out of stars shining in different colors. I felt that I wanted to be alone, and at the same time wanting to embrace another person.

Everything flowed and was fluid, the boundaries of myself became fuzzy. The feelings were peaceful, flowing, disconnected, detached and harmonic.

The experience lasted about 2-3- hours and gradually I felt myself returning to normal, and suffered no after-effects. Of course I was completely overwhelmed by the wonderful experience and could not logically believe or evaluate what I had seen and felt. I was very grateful to my friend for leading and guiding me into it, and told her so. It is worth pointing out that anyone who undertakes such an experience as the one I have just described above, should never do it without the presence of a qualified sitter or helper throughout.

ERNEST JONES

"Love, sex,-and marriage are 3 things that cannot be put in the same sack. Such a combination is dysfunctional"

A THOUGHT

"Sometimes you can't get <u>there</u> (where you want to go), from <u>here</u> (where you are now); and sometimes you have to move to another place (other than here), before you get there (where you want to go)".

C. Jung.- *"We don't solve our problems, we outgrow them".*

"THIS IS THE BRIGHT HOME..."

When I was married, in mid-life, for a number of reasons, I had come to the terminal decision to divorce my wife. It seemed that we had ended up in a situation which was, for me, no longer tenable. We did not agree in most things, and frequent disagreements interrupted our daily routine. I could not identify any way in which I could continue to grow, develop and enjoy life as I wanted, if I was to continue to remain married. I started looking for a suitable home to move into myself alone.

One Sunday afternoon taking a leisurely drive with a friend, he suggested we drive around a nearby small town in the mountains, which was supposed to be very quaint and appealing. So we took the drive there, and as we were driving up one of the hilly streets, we saw a house high above us among big oak trees that I thought very appealing and I pointed it out to my friend. As we turned the car around, I suddenly saw a "for sale" sign on its side. Something told me that that was the house I had been looking for.

Next day, on Monday morning I first called and then visited the realtor that was handling the sale. He told me that house had been built on an existing lot by a divorced lady with a young daughter, who had decided to sell the house and move to Colorado, because she was afraid her young daughter might become acquainted with some of the hippies that seemed to wander around that area at that time, and she was afraid that her daughter would become addicted to drugs in their company.

I immediately decided to buy that house and signed the sale contract that very day, without even seeing the interior of the house. It was one of the very best things I have done, because the price that I paid at that time was very reasonable, and as the years have gone by the area has turned out to be an extremely desirable area to live in, and the value of the house has multiplied many times over.

There was a peculiar historical quirk about the whole thing, however: when I bought it I thought I would move into it right away. Fate intervened: shortly after I had bought it, and before I had moved into it, the company I was working for decided to transfer me from California to the East Coast, and I agreed, so I never could really move into my dream house, and had to keep it rented to tenants for more than 12 years, until I could eventually retire to California and finally inhabit it.

In the years I have lived here, the house has been increased in size, with the addition of several rooms, bathrooms, and terraces, so it is now a very livable, comfortable house, very much to my liking. I would not wish to move to or live anywhere else.

It reminds me of that section of David Whyte's poem "The House of Belonging" which recites:

"This is the bright home,
In which I live
this is where
I ask
my friends
to come
this is where I want
to love all the things
It has taken me so long
to learn to love
This is the temple

of my adult aloneness
and I belong
to that aloneness
as I belong to my life
There is no house
like the house of belonging".

UNQUESTIONED SELF ASSURANCE!

"Why are you crying, if you have me?"

THE INVISIBLE THEATER.- (1998-2007)-(AGE 66-75)

One of my good friends was a prolific painter of large images of men and we had organized an exhibit of his pictures in a nearby location, and had invited a list of people to come see the exhibit. It was very successful and he sold some paintings. The paintings were very forceful and inspiring and depicted males in their full power, often based on mythological settings, but also quite realistic. We began to discuss the ways in which the paintings might be given a greater exposure to the public.

One of the ideas that came forth was the proposal to do a performance show with the paintings exhibited in a theatrical space, and also constituting a sort of 'frame' for the presentation, in other words using the paintings as part of the stories unfolding in the space. Some of us had recently attended a theatrical presentation of an imaginary tale and as a result, we put two and two together and conceived that a theatrical presentation could be constructed using imaginary tales applied to the painted figures. The idea seemed very promising, so using Peter Brook's description of a "Theater of the invisible" in his book "The Empty Space", we invited a few friends as actors and prepared for the first presentation of "The Invisible Theater" which took place in a small theatrical venue for an attendance of men only, shortly thereafter. It was a great success, so much so we decided to continue it in successive years and did so for 10 years between 1998 and 2007, with different programs to increasing audiences, and wildly enthusiastic acceptance. Most of the presenters and directors were not professional actors or directors or theater people. The position of director was rotated each year and the actual content of the pieces around each yearly theme was largely left up to the imagination and creativity of the presenters, each of whom wrote their own scripts. Costumes, props and theatrical staging were also largely left up to each individual presenter and his helpers, within some general guidelines. The subject matter of the presentations was designed to appeal specifically to men, with emphasis on mythology and archetypes, history, and from the individual imagination of the presenter. As can be seen by the following titles of the successive presentations, using these subjects, each presentation was to be designed by the actual men taking part as actors, with a different leader to be elected each year.

Announcements and invitation were sent out to a number of friends. This was going to be a presentation by men, for men only. A very moderate admission ticket price was to be asked from attendees.

In alignment with the "manly" orientation of the project, the question then became: what to select of the title/name of each pre-sentation? The eventual titles of the ten yearly presentation were:

1998.- "Archetypes of Man"
1999.- "Rumi Poems"
2000.- "Myths of Ancient Greece"
2001.- "Journey Through the Tarot"
2002.- "The 12 Signs of the Zodiac"
2003.- "Fairy Tales Re-Touched"
2004.- "Men: the Animal Spirits Within Them"
2005.- "A Hero's Journey"
2006.- "Men: their Dreams and Desires"
2007.- "Alchemy between Men"

The Invisible Theater had few rules but two guiding principles: 1) Create an shared experience about an important issue in your life today, to be presented by men to men, and 2) Any man is welcomed to participate, and to ask for help when needed, and to help others when asked.

What unified the group was a common demand to know ourselves better and to keep seeking answers. As we kept looking deeper for answers, learning to trust ourselves and other fellow seekers along this path, we grew closer. Some rare, authentic moments were on full display during an evening of the Invisible Theater, and that is what kept us returning year after year for ten consecutive events, with many new participants added to the group as time passed.

As the complexity if the presentations grew, we found that we had to start laying out the groundwork for each September show no later than the beginning of that same year, with meetings of the actors at least every month thereafter in order to properly prepare for the actual September presentations. The meetings were to work out the infinite details of putting the show together, but in fact, they became gatherings much more important than just theatrical rehearsals: they became meaningful social gatherings of a group of men not only engaged in a specific theatrical performance but something with a far greater importance: to have an ideal setting to form and reaffirm friendships, a place to meet new men of similar interests, a way to relate to other men under a highly purposeful and imaginative setting, and a milieu to learn and develop new forms of expression.

That theatrical experience had a direct beneficial effect upon many of the participants because it led them to be personally exposed to a public audience, an event not usually available to many, as well as affording each the chance to delve deeply into the meaning of their own individual lives. As an organizer, I was also deeply affected by the experience, and it resulted in multiple new friendships that are 'alive-and-kicking 'even to this day.

As one participant explained: "It felt as a new language I needed to learn—a decade of intense exploratory sacred brotherhood. I remember that 'words' were the things we tried to avoid in our performances. The Invisible Theater then was the place to escape the tendency to over-explain. The evenings became a refuge from life's incessant 'blah, blah, blah'. Instead there was an abundance of rare and raw moments. There was the 'cracked-open' beauty of men in their vulnerability and strength. Together, we opened up a realm of direct experience and moreover—direct initiation. And we had a lot of fun!

It turned out to be an immensely creative engagement for all of the men who participated, as actors and even as audience. The project very positively affected the lives of all of us.

Many of us have found out many years later, that the friendships formed at that time between us have endured, and indeed deepened, with the passage of time; that would not so easily have happened without the existence of the "Invisible Theater"

I wrote down the origin, start-up and eventual development of the project in a book I edited: "The Invisible Theater".

> **Cavoli Riscaldati (Italian slang).-** Literally: "reheated cabbage". Translation:. "The result of attempting to revive an unworkable relationship."

> **Amazonian Myth**.- "Man climbed a vine so high into the sky that eventually the bottom part of the vine broke off and he could not descend back to Earth using it. He climbed the vine because of disagreements with his wife, jealousy, envy of others, etc. He then became suspended in the air for all eternity, and eventually became the Moon. This is what happens when mankind loses touch with the Earth."

BASIC ESSENTIALS TO FOLLOW IN PADDLING (IE: LIVING YOUR LIFE, CONSIDERED IMAGINATIVELY AS PADDLING YOUR CANOE DOWN A RIVER)

When you are travelling down a river, paddling your canoe, (living) there are several items you must be aware of:

- It is easier to paddle <u>with</u> the flow. Back-paddling against the current is not a good idea, except in extreme emergencies.
- Paddling to the <u>side</u> of the river is generally not productive: you tend to get caught in whirlpools by the river's edge, which makes you go round and round.
- Realize that you <u>must</u> paddle. You can't stay put. You have to move down river. If you stay put, nothing happens. You would be half, (if not fully) dead). Staying put is not an option.
- Of course, one choice is to get in the boat and just <u>drift</u> downriver without paddling. The problem then is that you are at the mercy of the current. If you don't have a plan, you invariably become part of someone else's plan.
- Paddling <u>too hard and fast</u>, is risky. Slow down.

MARK TWAIN

"Good friends, good books, and a sleepy conscience: this is the ideal life".

THE MERCHANDISE MART.- A STORY

You go to the merchandise mart...... and buy <u>you</u>......*you buy* <u>yourself</u>.

Some time passes and you come to realize that you really don't like yourself.

So you go back and complain and call the manufacturer (God) and say you are not satisfied with yourself and complain to him for having made defective merchandise. Someone answers the phone saying "This is the Creation Dept." You state your case and the other party refers you, in a supercilious voice, to the "Whining Department", but warns you that sadly, they only have an answering machine that is programmed to erase your message (prayers) as soon as you hang up. You are not happy with that suggestion and say that you want to talk to the Customer Service Dept. You are then impatiently told that that department used to exist a long time ago but was discontinued many years ago. You begin to get steamed up about this and ask what is the company's return policy, whereupon you are promptly told that they don't accept returns and there is no return policy. If you bought the merchandise, you keep it, period.

Then you ask for the Parts Dept. thinking that in case they don't do repairs, maybe you can repair yourself, if they can supply you with the necessary parts (this is called "bargaining with God". You are peremptorily advised that there is no Parts Dept. and no spare parts are available, and that if you buy some in the used-parts aftermarket, that won't work, because each appliance is built with individually designed parts that fit only that particular unit. You get desperate and demand to talk directly to the President. They put you through to the President's office, but someone there who answers, tells you that the president hasn't been seen there for many eons of time. At that point you just give up in disgust, and go back and accept yourself as you are, and decide to do whatever changes you can do yourself, to yourself.

OSCAR WILDE

> *"The difference between literature and journalism is that journalism is unreadable, while literature is not read."*

> *"The famous Darwinian principle of the survival of the vulgarest, is absolutely true."*

SENIORITY
(2007+) (Ages 75+)

This particular period, that I am calling seniority, seems to have three unexpected saving graces, which I seem to be enjoying fully, and I recommend anyone else at this stage to recognize, respect and enjoy them. This is so even more if, as in my particular case, one enjoys reasonably good health and mobility, and is not troubled by constant visits to doctors or hospitals. For sure, I have had some heart troubles, but I still eat well, sleep well, can drive safely, and go about the business of living without major stress. I stay within a close perimeter of home, do not travel extensively (I have been to just about every place on the planet I wished to see anyway). And I do not wish at all to travel to those I haven't seen, because to my mind, they are not worth seeing!

The first "grace" is that at this time of my life, I feel that I have seen a lot, and gone through a lot, and have a wealth of accumulated experience. This provides a significant advantage: having few doubts, that is that I have a firm understanding of what I like and what I do not like, what I think is right and what I think is wrong; namely, my mind is made up and this provides significant relief. If someone disagrees with my views, I respect them and do not quarrel, but by the same token I have no qualms about expressing my own.

The second "grace" is having a definite view of God, the afterlife, and religion. After much investigation in my earlier years, reading opinions, participating in groups, I have eventually become an agnostic: that is to say that I realize and confess my inability as a human being to determine the existence of any God and of another world after death. This is not being an atheist, which means not believing in anything exists up there, no, it is simply believing that the mystery of the divine is too complicated and esoteric to be understood by human beings, and in fact, is not designed to be understood by us.

The above considerations invariably lead to my third "grace" which is the conclusion that it is pointless to worry about death, and what will come after, if anything, so it provides me with a great relief because I spend no time at all in wondering or worrying about such matters, and am content to experience whatever will happen then, when it happens.

For millennia, fear of death has been an essential factor in humanity's thinking, and many, many saviors, religious icons, churches, and organizations of all kinds have been created, often with atrocious records of sheer cruelty, abuse and murders of non-believers. In varying manifestations, this continues to the present day. So I have absolutely no faith or trust in any church or religious organization of any kind, which pretends to descend from some pretended savior or to have direct and exclusive access to a divine portal. In a sense, their existence has been always due to the unending desire of human beings for meaning, to understand and comprehend where we all came from and to where we will be going after death. It seems to me to be much simpler if one accepts the fact that such questions are beyond our human understanding and that we will not find answers to them. It seems to me to br much better to simply accept that fact and try to live this life as happily and as correctly as one can, without hurting any other life form and making the world we live in better, in any way we can. I consider assuming this attitude to be great gift to myself.

On Regrets.- by Jonathan Young

"A memory comes of a very successful friend who once asked for ideas on how to live so that, at the end, he would have no regrets. I thought long and hard, then answered that I thought regrets were inevitable. There isn't time to do everything. There is always some grief about all of the good ideas we never get around to developing. I don't think life has to be perfect to be fulfilling. I suggested that he give some thought to how to handle regrets well, rather than putting too much energy into avoiding them"

While I agree with most of Jonathan Young's statements above, I think he addresses only the type of regret dealing with <u>not</u> <u>having done something that could have been done and was not.</u> In doing so, however, he ignores the much more hurtful and piercing regret of <u>having done something which should NOT have been done</u>!. I certainly have a few of these in my life, and they have not been easy to handle. Over the long run, however, I believe that regrets about our past are the equivalent of useless cargo which is impeding present travel and should best be dumped by the wayside as soon as possible. There is nothing to be done about regrets—what is past, is past—and devoting any attention to them is a waste of time and leads nowhere. It s much more productive to devote that time to the present, and to do something about it that will improve our state of mind.

On Loquaciousness

(OR GARRULITY, OR EFFUSION,
OR...... JUST SIMPLY...... WORDINESS...)

Languages have often many words expressing roughly the same thing, in other words, synonyms can be abundant; but often, even if they can be defined as roughly equivalent, each synonym may imply slightly different meanings, with very delicate nuances that separate the individual words and give them a special twist of their own. The English language has often been characterized as being simple, direct, and in effect mincing no words, able to say something with fewer words than many of the romance languages. That is why it is claimed to be excellent for scientific or engineering texts: by its ability to concisely deal with abstract concepts in very few words.

That is one reason I enjoy the belief that if anyone cannot express a concept, no matter how abstract or complex, in plain, simple English, then there is really very little to say, perhaps to the extent that it should not be said at all. A sort of Occam's razor applied to language.

The above is an oversimplification of the facts, however, and in a sense, a contradiction, because English also has a very rich vocabulary of adjectives, especially in their slang variations, as I will attempt to show. This refers to the many forms of loquaciousness that can be described in English. For example, consider the incredibly rich list below, describing essentially different ways of saying "you are talking too much":

First we have the seven closely related cousins :and a twattler is an idle, trifling or tattling talker, not too different from:

To Babble, which means to utter inarticulate or meaningless sounds, to utter unintelligently, which is closely related to the action of

To Blather, which also means to speak or utter foolish talk or nonsense, and

To Jabber, meaning to speak rapidly, unintelligently or without making sense, or to make rapid nonsensical, unintelligible talk, as in the case of a

Twaddler, who is someone who talks foolishly and pretentiously, and engages in silly talk, and

To Twattle is to make foolish or trivial talk gossip,

To Rattle which is rapid and noisy talk, and a rattler is one who talks fast and furiously, and

To Prattle is to talk foolishly or like a child, issuing idle or foolish talk.

The above seven, in the family, are to be slightly distinguished from the three indiscreet triplets

To Blabber, which is to reveal or disclose indiscreetly, to prattle, to idle chatter, and not to be confused with "to Babble".

To Blab Off, which means to reveal a secret, to say what is better left unsaid, or to talk too much.

To Tattle, to be distinguished from **Twaddling** and **Twattling** above, is to gossip, to tell tales about others, to talk idle, to prate.

Referring to talking too much, we enter the terrain of:the twins:

To Gab is to talk especially glibly or excessively, and

To Gibber, which is to talk rapidly and incoherently, and of course to talk gibberish.

Then there are the "sound-generating" types of discourse, often compared to sounds animals make, (we are now entering the zoo) such as:

> **Chatter**, which means to talk rapidly or trivially, or to utter a rapid series of short, inarticulate sounds, as a squirrel, which is a close relative of **Natter** which means more or less the same thing, and

> **To Gabble**, which is to talk quickly or incoherently, to utter rapid cackling sounds as geese, (*we are moving into the barnyard now*) or to make glib, incoherent, or foolish talk, or

> **To Cackle**, meaning to make a shrill, broken cry, as a hen that laid an egg, or to utter in a cackling manner, or to emit a short, shrill laugh (*hopefully short!....... we can't keep up with that sort of thing for too long; it makes everyone too nervous*). We can more easily deal with:

> **Clacking**, (*to be distinguished from **Cackling** seen above to relate only to poultry and hencoops*) which is to make a short, dry sound as two flat pieces of wood striking together, but also to chatter heedlessly, to utter unthinkingly. No chickens involved here.

There are also some wet variations of the subject that are:

> **To Drivel**, is to let saliva flow from the mouth, to slobber, to talk foolishly and to make senseless talk, and

> **To Slobber**, meaning to ooze wet and foul, with liquids oozing from the mouth, and to talk or

act gushingly, and its nearly identical relative **To Slabber**, which redundantly is to slobber or drivel.

There are also some delicious compound forms such as:

To Gibble-Gabble and To Bibble-Babble, which seem to been in use around 1901, but have gone into obscurity since, because there seems to be no exact definition of what they meant, so one has to invent a precise meaning; it shouldn't be too hard to do, especially for a good chatterer.

If one is babbling at very low volume, so that no one can under-stand what one is saying, then one is **Mussitating**, which means: "to mumble, or to mutter".

Finally there are some action-packed utterances, which are:

To Rant, meaning to speak in loud, violent or extravagant language, to declaim vehemently, to rave, to frolic noisily, to be uproariously jolly, to utter declamatory and bombastic talk (*don't we all enjoy a bit of that?....*) and

To Rave, to speak loudly or incoherently or with extravagant enthusiasm.

One can see the richness or the language in the availability of multiple ways of describing the whole business of excessive, foolish or silly talk. Time to stop; I don't want to be too short of words, but in the other hand, if I continue, we would be engaging in excessive **patter** and **jabber**, and be considered nothing but **windbags**, prone to **grandiloquence**.

Which reminds me of the time my friend Nicholas said....... Oh! well......... as the very **voluble** would say: that is another story...... I mustn't get too **verbose** here or **long-winded;** otherwise, I would be accused of **blowing smoke** and **spouting forth** with uncontrollable **logorrhea.** Some people, you know, consider **glibness** (meaning being too fluent, often thoughtlessly, superficially, or insincerely), a social misdemeanor. But it is much worse than just a minor social misbehavior, not to mention a bore; it is almost in the same undesirable class as being **prolix**! The latter must be avoided at all costs. That is what happened the time two friends and I went down to the beach and.........but I am again going off on more **gossip**!

It is important, of course, in this on-going **holding-forth** on synonyms, to stick to the basic principles of simple, direct English, and avoid **sermonizing** and **expatiating**, the unmistakable signs of those that with poor breeding, and worse taste, indulge in senseless **speechifying** or for that matter, **spouting forth** as well. Also, even plain **prating** will never do, either. There is a risk that we might call upon ourselves the babbling curse, which in the Harry Potter books and movies causes the cursed to continue babbling forth without stopping. We simply must not continue to **jaw, rap, twaddle**, ... or tattle?....or is it **twattle**?...or...well...take your pick! But by no means ever allow yourself to continue to **gush** at length, or to **mussitate** too much, for the benefit of your friends, and society at large.

At this point, a good friend from a state in the deep South, with a pronounced southern drawl, will say that "I should shut my pie hole!"

Finally, at the risk of sounding too **multiloquent**, I should admit that, as one wit exclaimed, I have missed, in the above comments, an excellent opportunity to keep my mouth shut.

Sources:---*Standard College Dictionary. Harcourt, Brace &World. 1963*
      —*Dictionary of American Slang. Wentworth and Flexner. 1975*
      —*Roget's Thesaurus.*

PARACELSUS.- *"Alterius non sit, qui suus essere potest"*

Be not another, if you can be yourself

GANYMEDE VARIATIONS

For whatever reason, he ancient Greek myth of Ganymede has always attracted me, and over the years I have collected a series of stories and fables relating to that myth. Finally, I put all of these together in the paragraphs below. I already published these as one of the items in another book I wrote: "Hypomnemata", published by Xlibris, but this story has been so meaningful to me, that I wanted to include it again in this volume:

"It is a well-known ancient Greek myth: that of Ganymede, young Phrygian prince, son of King Tros of Troy, a sire of that accursed dynasty whose family history has become so engrained into the mythological matrix of our culture.

Ganymede was young and relatively inexperienced, but he had three superior attributes: he was *beautiful*, the most beautiful; mortal known in his time; he must have been in one way *ready* for his fate; finally he the *courage* and will power to accept it graciously.

He was shepherding his flock of sheep one sunny day on the slopes of Mount Ida, when a great shadow engulfed him, cast by an enormous bird, an eagle with huge wingspan, large beak and power beyond measure. It was no other than Zeus himself, in the form of a monstrous raptor who swooped down upon surprised Ganymede, and in a whirlpool of feathers, dust, and wind, engulfed him in a mysterious fog, lifted him, and took him away through the clouds and the high Grecian sky to the palaces on Mount Olympus, legendary home of all the Gods.

The story says that Zeus in his godly visions had spotted and become enamored of the winsome beauty of the young prince, and as liege, exercised his will upon the boy. We are such toys in the hand of the Gods!

What happened there, on that day, on that sunny slope, is still unclear: Was there any advance notice or at least forebodings on the part of Ganymede? Was it possession, abduction, perhaps even rape? Was Ganymede unconsciously longing for an epiphany of this sort? In the same way young men have sometimes unthinkingly longed for wars as decisive arbiters of their path, as a way to escape the tormenting question of what to do with their lives? Adrenalin builds up at such momentous times and electric charges invite divine interventions. How many of us have longingly wished for that incredible point in time when the old life falls back, flashes of lightning appear (Zeus again!), a momentous calm invades us, our vision clears, and our lives move on in a completely different direction: we grow, we expand, we are someone else, with new outlooks, new perspectives. Often all it takes is a word, a loving phrase, a casual encounter, a teacher, a mentor, and we are forever changed.

The abductor comes down in the form of an eagle, the only bird capable of withstanding, undamaged, the proximity of Zeus's deadly lightning bolts made for him in the chthonic forges of Hephaistos. The eagle might have been Zeus's *ka*, or other self as well, just as a solar hawk descended upon the Pharaohs at their coronation. The flash of the divine has to come upon us not only when we are ready, and have the courage, but it also has to come in the right form.......in this case, the 'eagle'. Animal forms are so much easier for us to assimilate when spirit epiphanies take place. So Gods often appear to us in the shape of animals. We would not be able to comprehend anything if it were to witness the awesome appearance of raw divinity undisguised.

How tempting to imagine that after all, there has to be complicity between God and mortal, between Zeus and Ganymede. It seems that men, as they grow, need this completion, this mutual initiation, this sparking of the circuits between each other, before they can be whole.

Ovid, in his "Metamorphoses" gives it a pregnant twist. He says "Jupiter found another shape preferable to his own" in one translation; in another even better one:

> "The King of the Gods once loved a Trojan boy named Ganymede; for once there was something found that Jove would rather be than what he was"

Not only does Ganymede have his beauty, origin of the whole episode, but he also has to be *ready* for what will happen. Seeds sown upon unfertile land do not germinate. We must be at the right place at the right time for epiphanies to happen. What in heaven's name has a poor mortal to do in order to prepare himself and be ready? Some knowledge helps, a familiarity with history, an awareness of himself, an open mind and heart, willingness to listen, and above all to sense steadfastness in soil and body, a certain willingness to stretch, tempered by self-respect, and an innocent sense of self-worth devoid of the incursion of affairs of the ego.

How many modern corporate "Zeuses" have spotted likely young candidates within their organizational ranks, and have extended protective wings over their careers, nursing tem while preparing them for future increased responsibility—but only if the candidates are ready: naiveté, innocence, immaturity, excessive idealism, inflation, wayward romanticism, are all obstacles that encumber that readiness.

How many mentors, fathers, teachers, family friends, have "swooped down" on promising youths at the right time and so changed their lives, taking them away from the shade of the family tree into the full light of the sun! How many young 'abducted' men have taken a turn before the materialization of their planned futures as perfect husbands, with perfect wives, perfect jobs, in perfect little towns and have instead followed their bliss (or Zeus's).

Ganymede was tending his flock of sheep, meek animals that stand for passivity, tranquility, placidity, protection: an environment that implies safety, continuity, and security. That, in the midst of a universe which by any measure is known to be a constantly changing plasma of particles, waves, chaotic energy, entropic displacements, at the opposite end of the scale from "sheep' values. Our Ganymede would stay stuck in his grassy slope forever if the whirlwind of feathers, dust and power had not forever changed his life. That the abduction might have included rape, not in the literal sense, but metaphorically, does not sound farfetched in this context. Do we not forcibly have to be taken away, 'raped away', invaded, penetrated by the radically new in order to leave behind our sheepish inclinations and take our place among the stars? It is appropriate then that these transitions take place in a state of turbulence, sometimes perceived as life-threatening. As in modern chaos theory, where 'chaotic attractions' or systems in a state of agitation, display at once features of chaos and features of order, we must go through this layer of agitated energy before we come to new states of being. Ilya Prigogine, 1977 winner of the Nobel prize for chemistry, discovered that transition to a higher state of energy is *universally* accompanied by turbulence. He says "…it is at such vibrating times that living systems (humans, chemical solutions, whole societies) are shaking themselves to higher ground. It appears that ancient Greeks had it all figured out thousands of years ago. So why make a fuss about a metaphorical rape by the divine? Should we not consider it an opportunity? Greece at that time must have been a culture of warriors, thinkers, and shepherds. A culture of shepherds needs a myth of glory. Shepherding as a life can be difficult and boring. This is probably why the Ganymede myth became so popular at that time. It offered a promise of transcendence. This is far more understandable than to attribute its popularity only to be justified by same-sex lifestyles in the ancient world.

Ganymede had one last attribute, however: besides putting up a fight, as we can imagine he had done, no matter how uneven the forces; he must have had the *courage* to willingly, at last, agree to his abduction.

It took courage at first to fight and to, subsequently, say yes to the force, which would pull him up to a higher state of being, as an electron is bounced to a higher orbit when struck by energy. Perhaps, after all, he was not that surprised to see the eagle. He may have been waiting for it all along, hardly daring to believe he would be so fortunate as to be chosen, and wondering if he would have the courage to face it when it came.

In Seattle, Washington, in the beautiful Pacific Northwest, there is a well known 'fish ladder', artificially constructed to allow spawning salmon to return to their native waters where they were born. The fish come up in great numbers against then locks and dams, but they find their way around those by the 'fish ladder' a contrivance of escalating kevels, with waters pouring down. The salmon follow the smell of the fresh water cascading down and follow the fish ladders up, where they face two choices: they can either leap out of the water, landing on the next higher step of the ladder, or else they can face square openings in the weirs and dams on the ladder itself and swim through these holes against the current and on to the next step. One can see the square openings from behind a series of glass panels set up for observation. The openings themselves are foreboding. It is dark inside and nothing can be seen of what is behind them. The fish that choose that route approach the openings, and for a minute stand before them motionless, just holding their place against the current. You can imagine them consciously wavering for a moment before taking the final plunge through the darkness into God knows what! A fish trap? A dead end? Open jaws? Something worse? or perhaps the way of delivery to the Promised Land and the garden of delights. It seems as if there was a Ganymede in every salmon. He followed his call and reached, like them, his final destiny, with great courage.

Then Ganymede, the story goes on, became Zeus's lover and was appointed to be cup-bearer to the Gods, given eternal youth, and made immortal. Not quite baubles, but very big gifts. Gifts transform the youth into a man, and then into a semi-God. His beauty, his readiness, and his courage got him there. A final gift came when Zeus, in spite of the jealous rages of his sister and wife, Hera, placed Ganymede among the stars as the constellation Aquarius, the cup-bearer, which in time became the water-bearer in the familiar image of a male figure carrying a water pitcher or cup over his shoulders from which water pours out.

To be sure, it wasn't water that he was serving on Olympus, nor even wine, but nectar and ambrosia, drink and food of the Gods. But generations of ascetics and prohibitionists perhaps transformed the 'wine' into water, and into the 'watery' astrological depiction that has come down to our time.

If we consider a broader view of Ganymede as Aquarius, some eloquent meanings begin to appear: what Ganymede/Aquarius is pouring out of his cup is more than just water, or nectar and ambrosia.

He is really pouring out the 'overflow' of his fulfilled and realized life, his excess energy and vitality to those around him, including you and me, because he is in the heavens above every night pouring his own soul and his own being to the Earth and humanity below. He is a true cupbearer, who pours the overflow of his own vital energy into others.

In the Tarot cards, card number 17 is 'The Star', seen as a figure pouring the waters of life and universal love. Again, it refers to Aquarius/Ganymede, a sign associated with peace, love and inspiration, although the figure is usually represented as female. A Jungian interpretation is that the Aquarius figure is the soul of Ganymede, his anima, the flower of his soul, his female consciousness, which has opened to make everything conscious within itself. He has nothing left which is unconscious; a shining star in the dark sky.

But the Ganymede story can be reversed, with a poignant meaning: assume that it is older Zeus himself who is tending sheep on the slopes on Mt. Olympus, a king without a crown, entrapped in a life of tranquil domesticity and habit, lulled by memories, set routine, reminiscences of former kingly glory, perhaps partly engineered by wily Hera, and partly by himself, far removed from the hurling of thunderbolts, and poorly warmed by a smoldering, smoky fire which provides but little heat. Not too different from the situation in which some older men find themselves in their 'golden years'. We get old because we tell ourselves that we must act and think old. It is safer to bask in safety, remembrance, and even nostalgia, than to face the risks of the present and ever-uncertain future.

Assume further, for a moment, that it is Ganymede who swoops down on slow-moving Zeus with a burst of youthful energy, creativity, explosive passion, forward-facing plans, and then shakes up Zeus and bounces him to a much higher energetic state. Is that a meaningful story? When the birth of a new son, the friendship of a young man, or the passion of one, succeeds in displacing the clouds of passivity and restores the older Zeus to vigor, and to play in the fields of the Gods, once again sitting in his abandoned throne? Does it sound improbable that a silly, naïve Ganymede could do so much for the king of the Gods? Not at all. All men sometimes notice an eruption of the energy of the eternal boy within them, the Puer Aeternus, a voice that refreshes, rejuvenates, vitalizes their outlook, introducing new imaginative and creative ideas into their perspective and wonder where it came from. And who says Ganymede had to be naïve and silly? Youth is not necessarily either, and its capacity to bring new life and new breath is immense. In one of his ecstatic poems, Rumi says:

> *"By a single thought that comes into the mind, in a single moment a hundred worlds are overturned"*

These two were lucky, in fact, because in either case the affair comes to a successful resolution. There is closure. Reality is often less favoring: the lover may not always meet the beloved at the right time. In the words of Thomas Hardy:

> *"In the ill-judged execution of the well-judged plan of things, the call seldom produces the comer, the man to love rarely coincides, with the hour of loving"*

My friend Jim C., an inveterate weaver of tales, says Aquarius had a particular significance in relation to Ganymede and the Aquarian Age. One can reasonably postulate that the Old Testament personae were essentially shepherds. Abraham was a shepherd who was asked by God to sacrifice his shepherd son Isaac, by that terrible Yahweh, the jealous and demanding God ruling over what was essentially a shepherds' tribal form of human organization. In that way of life there was an ever-present patriarchal God that told you what you had to do. A finger-pointing, accusatory God who was the arbiter and final judge. You did nothing but obey his commands…. commandments……if you wanted to belong. It was the age of Aries, the ram. Almost everybody was a wandering shepherd or nomad.

He says that the coming of Jesus opened up and softened the rigor of the Old Testament injunctions. We then had the Age of Pisces (the watery, fluid time). Jesus, the fisher of men, symbolized as a fish, did not point fingers, but said we all have a relationship with God (who is still 'the Father', however) and appoints himself as the intermediary between man and the divine. There is a curious story in the later Gospels that says when Jesus invited the apostles to the last supper; he gave them directions to the house where the meal was going to be held. The directions were simply to go into town and follow the man 'carrying water' (Aquarius and Ganymede again!) who would lead them to the appointed place. A man carrying water would have been an unusual sight in those times because carrying water was considered to be the job of women. No self-respecting man of that time would 'carry water', unless he was a slave. Yet, they were asked to follow the water-carrier, who was easily spotted by the aware, by those who were ready, and had the courage to follow him to the appointed place.

The spirit of the coming Age of Aquarius goes further and says: man himself is divine and a spark of star-stuff resides in the heart of each one of us. That is why Zeus raised Ganymede to Olympus and gave him immortality, as if saying Ganymede himself is partly divine, and there is no need for intermediaries. All we have to do to remind ourselves of this is to look up in awareness at the night sky. Ganymede in a sense becomes Zeus and Zeus becomes Ganymede. The 'wine' (nectar and ambrosia) in the Olympic feast turns to water in the Aquarian jar. It is the watercarrier-server Ganymede who is to lead us to the new age. Let us not forget in any case what that jar originally contained.

So far, this story develops in an ever-increasing spiral of positive meaning, and all appears to 'end well' in the Hollywood style. But there is another darker and endlessly woeful possible denouement as well. Suppose that Ganymede, for whatever reason, was not ready and did not have the courage to accept his destiny when it came. We can trivially assume in the story, that when the eagle approached, Ganymede ran for cover to the house of his father, hid in a cave, and even worse, did not see or even recognize the eagle as it appeared before him, as we often deny reality by pretending it isn't there, mostly because we are afraid of it. By doing so, he might have remained in a life of safety, without creativity, security without spirit, inertia instead of action. What a waste of opportunity and talent! Yet this is the choice of millions of young man when the numinous comes knocking at the door.

And much, much worse and far more painful: assume for a moment that in the reverse story, it is Zeus who ignores and does not see Ganymede when he appears and irrupts into Zeus's domestic, loveless life of settled hearth and home. By that blindness in a crucial moment, Zeus would forsake the spark of youth, and life, and love, and beauty, and remain an endless, unrealized potential, forever despairing, unmanifest, and undeveloped. What insanity! The price he pays (that many pay) for blindness and insensitivity at the moment of truth is enormous, beyond calculation. It can be the closest thing to a sentence of spiritual and emotional death. Shakespeare puts it well:

> *"There is a tide in the affairs if men,*
> *which taken at the flood leads on to fortune,*
> *omitted, all the voyage of their life*
> *is bound in shallows and in miseries*
> *and we must take the current when*
> *it serves or lose our ventures"*

The eagle is an important symbol for the souls of royalty as well. A dark interpretation of Ganymede's ascent to heaven as an eagle, would be that he himself, not Zeus, was the eagle, As in the ancient Greek tradition where kings were allowed to reign for no more than one hundred months, to be replaced as titular king by their heir or a selected young man, who was then sacrificed after his one day of kingship (and his soul ascended to heaven as an eagle?) The original king would then come back, marry his widowed daughter-in-law, since the throne passed through matrilineal descent and resume another hundred months of reign. The story of Abraham and Isaac lies in this same general vicinity. So perhaps the story of Ganymede was the story of one more sacrifice?

There is an important twist to this story. The myth says that to mitigate the loss of his son, Zeus sent King Tros a gift of two twin horses that could gallop over water, although in other versions, the gift is also described as a golden vine. We are given to understand that the king was satisfied with his gift(s) and did not cause further trouble. At first pass, it would seem that the father was somewhat callous after all, two horses only, or one simple vine, even if it was golden, in exchange for his exceptional son? Should he not have grieved more? demanded more? Actually, the king was a wise man: he did not insist in Ganymede forever tending sheep and remaining a boy, when the doors of his destiny as a man opened up. He was wise to realize what was happening and to let go of his son, when fate and revelation knocked at his door. Good fathers cannot keep their sons in captivity forever.

There is a wicked, irreverent version of the Ganymede story written bt Anthony Young, where he has imaginary Ganymede give *his* version of the story:

"When I spotted the stranger, I figured him to be a good catch, so I put on my best innocent/seductive pout......Noble, undoubtedly. Rich, too....Just the ticket for a young prince with scant prospect of an inheritance... So I made the first coy moves... But I wasn't ready for the self-assurance with which he responded: I had never met a man like this! ...And so, after a few initial moves, it was I, not he, who was dizzy with desire. Of course, I didn't know then that he was the immortal Zeus All-Father: not until he begged me to go home with him to Olympus ......then I wept with terror....but he assured me he would put me in a safe place...then he offered to fly me there on the back of an eagle...how could I refuse?......so I arrived here on Olympus. Life among the Gods is challenging, but the love of the All-Father makes it all worthwhile. Now I could never go back to the vacuous life of a mortal. Praise Zeus!"

Isn't this a story of the young and the old as two sides of the same coin? William Empson says that the early Egyptians had only one hieroglyph to depict both 'young' and 'old'. So that an Egyptian looking at a baby, would also at the same time think of an old man. They showed which of the two was meant by an additional hieroglyph, not to be pronounced, which may have taken the place of a gesture in conversation. Only later did they learn to separate the two sides of the antithesis. The notion of age excites conflict in almost all who use it: between recognizing the facts about oneself, and feeling grown-up or feeling still young and strong.

Isn't that the real tension between Zeus and Ganymede?

The Ganymede story has also much wider implications, and here is Goethe speaking about romantic love using Ganymede as his theme, in an original verse, from which I copied selected lines from a French translation of the original German:

> "Dans ton sein
> je repos et je languis
> et tes fleurs et tes herbes
> se present sur mon coeur.
> La haut me porte mon elan
> les nouages s'inclinent
> vers la terre, les nouages
> se penchent vers l'amour nostalgique
> vers moi, vers moi"

which I translated into English below:

> *"Upon your breast,*
> *I rest and I languish*
> *and your flowers and your herbs*
> *press against my heart*
> *the clouds are poised*
> *towards the Earth, the clouds*
> *go towards nostalgic love*
> *towards me! towards me!"*

Again quoting Anthony Young:

> *"If your business is with the Gods, ponder not these trifling concerns of mortals. Ganymede's beauty is not lost to us: let your gaze ponder the stellar sky of the summer night, where the cupbearer still pours for all to see and drink, if you will, of the nectar".*

Robert Graves says that the name Ganymede comes from the Greek "ganuesthai" and "medea", meaning "rejoicing in virility". Was it not that what Ganymede and Zeus were doing?

A LIFE'S THEME

I have often wondered whether people's lives have a certain specific "theme" or main hue which colors most incidents in their history. As if each individual person's life was tinged by a special color or story which permeated most or all, episodes in it, and that it would be different from that of other human beings. The horoscope in fact does that in a way because each sign of the Zodiac has a particular set of qualities or properties associated with it, and persons born under each sign are said to be affected or possess those qualities.

In my experience I have found that to be generally true: for example some persons I have known have been always distinguished by traits such as: the love of music, or the attraction to animals, or their gentle and kind nature, or their ability to speak clearly, or their hostile and contentious nature, and so on. These preferences are notable in their day to day behavior and in their general comportment. These qualities also seem to be born with us; they are not acquired with time, but present at our very beginning.

In my case, what I have noticed is the feeling of wanting to be independent, ambitious but not reckless, searching for responsibility. These are associated with my native sign, Capricorn, the goat. So perhaps there is something to this idea, although I have never sought astrology's help in making any decision.

What I think is true is that writing anything about oneself is like embarking on a journey of self-discovery. The more one writes about our life, the more one discovers things about oneself that would not have been conscious before. It is like mining deep into the earth, to discover whatever gold or coal (or plutonium!) lies there.

AIM.- (FROM MATT HAIG, IN "NOTES ON A NERVOUS PLANET")

> *"To feel every moment, to ignore tomorrow, to unlearn all the worries and regrets and fear caused by the concept of time. To be able to walk around and think of nothing but the walking. To lie in bed, not asleep, and not worry about sleep. But just be there, in sweet horizontal happiness, unflustered by past and future concerns".*

A PROTEST ABOUT MEMORY

As I got older, especially in the most recent years of my life, I have found that my memories of events and incidents that happened to me, as well as of people whom I met, have significantly decreased and become less reliable over time. I seem to remember some very old instances, and seem to forget more recent ones. Names, locations, times, and happenings have gone with the wind, so to speak.

I want to file a protest about this (a lot of good will that do.......!!) because in the latter stages of life, one should be able to enjoy remembering those names and incidents as a repose and solace at the end of a long life, and instead we are deprived of them when they would help most.

I guess the moral of that story is that one should concentrate one's attention simply on the present: what is happening right now, and enjoy it at this very moment, and stop trying to remember what happened in the past.

Not a bad injunction!

ADVICE FROM HOROSCOPE FOR CAPRICORN IN TODAY'S NEWSPAPER

"You need to remind yourself more often that it's OK if life is easy.
Maybe it's your turn"

Not a bad instruction at all!

AND WHAT FOLLOWS?

When one reaches an advanced age as I have, the inevitable question arises; what happens when we die? Where do we go?

In the life I have experienced, I have come to the conclusion that it is an unanswerable question. Our limited human capacities are not sufficient to be able to answer that question. Yes, there is a very strong tendency, in all existing religions, to try to answer the question to alleviate anxiety, gather flocks of believers, and explain the unexplainable. In my view they are all but feeble attempts to tranquilize and reassure people without any proof of their assumptions. If one considers the amount of time, energy, and effort humanity has dedicated over its history to try to define what happens after death, one is amazed at the enormous amount of invention, without the slightest proof, that has been expended in this quest. All to no avail. The sad part of that history is to consider the enormous killings, mass murders, sacrifices and other oppressions which have been, and continue to be, inflicted upon humanity by these errant churches, organizations, and belief systems.

So, I am not an atheist who believes there is no God. I am simply an agnostic, who says 'I do not know' and will find out what really happens (or not!) when the time comes. As a corollary to this conviction, the conclusion is my belief that **YOU** don't know either, and that **NOBODY ELSE** knows either. The advantage of this position is that one does not have to spend sleepless nights wondering about those impossible questions. I have, therefore, more disposable time to employ in more productive engagements.

Lightning Source UK Ltd.
Milton Keynes UK
UKHW011825110822
407174UK00002B/723